SWEET GRASS

by

William A. Luckey

William A. Luckey

Published in 2011. For more information about other books by
William A. Luckey, please go to waluckey-west.com. The author
may be reached at waluckey@cybermesa.com.

to Fred Hartfield

William A. Luckey

Other books by William A. Luckey

Along Chico Creek/Fast Horses
Five Cent Return
Burn English
The English Horses
Nothin' Much
Unknown Friend

HISTORY

Horse owners have always wanted to know whose horse is the fastest. Speed has been contested since mankind first tamed the animal for transportation instead of food.

Before the late 1800's, on the formal tracks jockeys rode their horses in an upright position, toes down, whip in hand. Photos and artistic renderings show this erect and illogical manner of riding at speed.

On the Western plains, the American Indians raced their ponies riding bareback, knees drawn up and bodies leaned forward. Cowboys also indulged in man's need to find out who had the fastest horse, and some emulated the Indians by leaning as far forward as possible to encourage their mounts.

In 1887 a man named Willie Simms began what was to be a very successful career as a jockey; noted for his distinct style of racing with shortened stirrups and hunched over the horses' backs, Mr. Simms had great success in riding winners at the tracks in the East and in England, where his style of riding was called the 'monkey's crouch'. After returning to the United States, he won the United States riding title in 1894. In 1896, he won the Kentucky Derby aboard Ben Brush.

Tod Sloan is often mistakenly credited with this 'new' style of riding, taking it to England in 1897. Willie Simms may well have learned the style from a former slave, Abe Hawkins. The revolutionary style of riding later became known as 'the American' seat. Mr. Simms rode winners for several owners, including August Belmont, Jr., whose father gave his name to Belmont Park and the Belmont Stakes, now part of American racing's Triple Crown. Mr. Simms won the Kentucky Derby twice, the Belmont Stakes, and the Preakness, but not on the same horses. He is the only African-American jockey to win these three races.

Tod Sloan was inducted into the Jockey Hall of Fame in 1955; Willie Simms had to wait until 1977. Mr. Simms was of African heritage, while Sloan was a handsome white man of much charm and profligacy, dying broke in 1933 after losing his riding license in 1901.

While Willie Simms and August Belmont are real people; they have been placed where they fit best in the story. Although Mr. Simms rode for the Dwyer brothers until their partnership ended, he also rode for other owners. In wishing to resurrect the public's knowledge of this pioneer in racing, the author has more closely allied Mr. Simms with August Belmont. The author has admittedly taken great liberties with their individual personalities and all situations and incidents are purely imaginary. The rest of the characters in this book are solely the invention of the author.

ONE

Blue had to steady the light chestnut colt he'd just saddled, while two cowboys perched on the high fence yelled and slapped their legs, trying to stir up trouble. A third joined them, leaning over the fence and pounding the rail.

It was the first time Blue would ride the colt, and the youngster shuddered, ears frantically swiveling from Blue's soft words to the idiots yelling for action. Blue touched the sweaty neck as he swore under his breath. He didn't want a first buck from the youngster. Life was meant to be different for the blooded colt, not like the ranch stock that Blue usually rode.

When the trembling stopped and the colt's ears softened; when the chestnut shook all over with the saddle strings popping and the youngster didn't spook, then Blue knew it was all right for the moment.

In the quietest of movements, Blue held the end of the *mecate* knotted under the colt's jaw and walked to the fence. Without warning, he shoved the man standing on the rail backwards and of course the fall spooked the colt, who bolted until he hit the *mecate* knot and jerked his head. Blue cursed the stupidity that had forced his hand but there was only one way to shut the cowhands down; words would never have ended the raucous challenge.

Blue looked at the other two seated on the fence. "You want the same?" These were new men, Rhynes and Blake, unknown and unknowing, and Blue intended to set them straight from the beginning. If old man Norris were to the corrals, instead of laid up with a busted wing and broke ankle, all from this same terrified colt, then these boys'd be at their chores and not hooraying Blue and waiting for the fireworks.

The man lying flat to the ground, groaning some but in no hurry to move, he knew better. He'd been to the Norris spread for two years, hired on steady to a damned good job. Skippy he was known as, dumb fool name for a grown man, and no last name, which didn't much matter in the endless Nebraska sand hills.

Blue went back to the colt, looking down and away from the white-rimmed eyes. He very slowly coiled up the *mecate*, lacing its length across the palm of one hand while talking soft nonsense, muttering to himself about the damned foolishness of some men. Telling the colt that his tormentors were full size and still babies, still sucking on their mama's teat.

Now horses were honest, he said to himself, knowing full well those two rannies sitting on the rail were listening to the foolishness. All the while Blue talked, he was calming a high-bred colt that Con wanted broke easy to the bridle and accepting of human ways.

Horses fought back when they didn't understand, he said to the colt. They learned to trust a rider when their job was clear. Most were generous in a day's work, others sulled up when the job was rough and they were mistreated, but it was easy knowing what they were, how they acted. Men could fool each other and themselves too with their own words and actions until the real thing happened and it always did. A bad wreck, a man down and injured; only then the true heart and soul of a cowboy riding for the brand was known. It was why Blue chose horses since he'd been a half-broke youngster himself up in Wyoming.

He promised the chestnut colt that there'd be no more surprises, no more worrying. 'Leastways not from these fools; the one on the ground was up now, rubbing his backside and limping away. Muttering to himself but Blue sure as hell didn't care.

He stood to one side at the colt's head, playing with the tight lips, stroking the flat jowl as if there was nothing else needed doing. He stared into the big eye, noting that the brow was wrinkled, making the colt appear worried. It might be only physical, like two stockings or a wide blaze, but that eye, big and knowing, looked concerned right now, and eyes usually told the truth.

Three days ago Con Norris had thought to work the colt in the corral, nothing fancy, just a halter and lead and some circling, a whoa and a get-up but the colt panicked and ran over Norris, crippling the man for a month or longer.

There'd been a short and wide man with Con, a stranger and Con didn't tell the ranch hands who he was or what he was doing at the ranch. Norris went in to the corral and started fussing with the colt and Blue had wanted to speak his piece but the look to Norris' face, plus the wide man's steady glare, backed Blue off from making his opinion known. Words weren't easy for Blue, usually opening his mouth got him into trouble; this time he kept quiet and Con got run over by the colt, a handsome, long-legged three-year-old with fancy papers and obvious good breeding.

Later, after they got Norris to the house and sent a rider for the doc, Norris told Blue he wanted him and only him to work the colt, manner him as well as get him saddle-broke. "That son's the pure quill, Mitchell. Thoroughbred back far as those papers go. And he's got speed, you seen him to the horse trap. He can outrun anything I got here."

Blue nodded; the colt had been born the spring of '97, while Blue'd taken a band of geldings to Fort Robinson. He'd gone back that summer for a challenge, and came back slow in late fall, wounded in heart and body from a single horse race. A boy had died while Blue cradled his head, a boy he'd marked as a friend.

He brought with him one of the Norris geldings sold to the Army and ruined by callous men who saw money in the bay's defeat. The horse never fully recovered; Blue still used him for easy rides, sometimes ponying a youngster like the light chestnut, a good job for the bay and easy on Blue's old bones. Norris let the useless horse stay on the ranch, out of pity Blue figured, and maybe a soft heart well hidden by the rancher's bluff words.

Blue was a horse breaker past his prime. He'd been working the broncs for almost twenty years. First he'd been thrown out of school, then pulled away from what schooling his ma gave him, to work his own way. "You're a man now, you do a man's work." The words were as close to kind as anything his pa ever said to him. Then the old man took all Blue's earnings, said it was his due for siring the boy. Never did ask Blue if he'd wanted to be born.

Norris knew, even mean-tempered as he was, lying flat and hurting, he told Blue to take his time, use his way of starting the colt. "Don't listen to those damned fools I've hired. Hell, boy, when I get up from this bed there's going to be firing done around here."

Then Con laid his head back down and Blue studied the man. Con had gone old; face lined and weathered, the forehead white above burned skin. The wide shoulders were hunched even lying on the bed. The black hair had gone gray, then almost white, through the years Blue'd worked off and on for the Rafter Bar T. The dark blue eyes were changed too, the lids drooping, pink-lined, the gaze watery instead of hard and clear.

Blue hated what he saw in the aging process, 'specially in a man he'd come to admire and respect.

Con's great strength and purpose seemed shattered along with his ankle and wrist by a frightened colt that in the past would have been easy for Con to settle. Damn, Blue thought, seeing himself lying in that bed. Con owned something. Blue had nothing to his name except character and reputation, and a temper that got him in constant trouble.

A broke ankle and arm would kill him, holed up somewhere, a cave or protective trees, through a cold winter and he'd be a picked-clean skeleton before spring. Blue stepped back from the bed and Con's sad eyes; such thoughts would ruin him.

Blue and Connor Norris got along; they understood each other's ways and thoughts much as any two humans could, being as they were mavericks with a 'to hell with you' manner. It was this understanding, not the pay or the ranch setting, the food or the comfort of a decent bunkhouse, that made working full time for a rancher possible. Blue's life had been mostly riding an undetermined direction, landing at a ranch, getting paid per head and tackling the wild stock other bronc busters couldn't handle.

This chestnut colt, though, he deserved a better start than a saddle slapped on him, a rank cowhand spurring till the colt sulled and quit. Blue had confronted his boss on the colt, wouldn't start him before the chestnut turned three. Thoroughbreds were different, he told Con, and this one in particular had the makings to be something. They'd argued; Blue won.

Now Con Norris grinned when he spoke of the colt's breeding, said he had it in mind to send the colt back East for some racing, like they were doing at the big tracks, making money for the owner and trainer. He stared direct at Blue, who tightened instinctively.

He'd already guessed that the short and wide man, who disappeared soon as Con got put to bed, was some racing stable big shot out looking for horses, maybe even willing to buy the chestnut. The not knowing made Blue nervous, since he knew that Con had run a loss these past few years, with drought and grass fires taking graze and setting up a fierce worry.

For the colt it would be all about running fast as he could; what he was bred for and what he naturally wanted to do. It was Blue's job to teach him certain skills so that the colt could run in good company and win.

Then there was that bribe Norris hadn't thought to mention or even know its importance; a trip East to deliver the colt for a good price to some rich robber baron who got his money off coal miners or railroads and needed a winner to let him inside the circle of wealthy men who ruled the world. Blue laughed at himself, hearing his own voice make judgments about people he'd never met living in a world he'd never understand.

It was the trip East that scared him. Over a thousand miles, he figured. Or more, he didn't rightly know and wasn't going to ask Con and show any interest at all in the prospect. He'd traveled several thousand miles on horseback, maybe more, or less, but it had been in a big circle, from Wyoming to Arizona to Colorado, up into Nebraska again and took stops and starts and years to make the distance.

It was their world, not Blue's, not Con Norris's, but their world of riches and silver, lace and champagne and things Blue'd seen or read about but didn't think much on. That was what scared him. The not knowing, fumbling around like a street drunk in a place that had no use for him.

Except that he knew horses. And his son lived there, in one of those big cities. Despite Joshua Snow's terrible death in that Fort Robinson race, Blue still read about what was happening in the race world, who was winning, who'd lost a close contest. Con had been getting papers from the East; kept his mind busy he said, things he could think on. It was the reading in those papers made him try breeding a good stallion to a mare he'd bought cheap but she had those blue-blood, all-important papers.

Thinking on it now, Con's giving Blue these newspapers, saying that maybe he'd like reading them when the nights came early, now it made sense that Con had all this in mind, wanted to keep Blue interested, let him know what waited for him while he worked the colt.

Blue had to admit that the jockey, Willie Simms, and his unexpected win on Ben Brush in the Derby, had been something to think about and study. He'd read in the papers about that man, Willie Simms. That he was a Negro was of little concern; it was Simms' riding with his short stirrups and winning for a gent named Belmont that was the real interest for Blue. And another one, Tod Sloan, white so the newspapers made a big fuss about him going to England and showing the English how to ride, to perch up on a horse's neck and beat most every challenger. Simms too had been to England, rode against the best and won, but he wasn't much in the papers, it was more about the men whose horses he rode, Belmont and the Dwyer boys and Levy. Men who owned fancy horses and took their pleasure from winning.

Blue read about them when a newspaper got sent from Chicago or even New York. Con Norris was proud that he kept up with the world outside of his Valentine, Nebraska ranch set plumb square in the sand hills.

These world-known owners were the kind of men who both terrified and disgusted Blue. They bought their wins, they paid high dollar and got the applause and praise and some other son of a bitch had raised and trained the winning horse. And a man like Willie Simms won the race for the indulgent owners.

It was the spring of nineteen hundred, a whole new century to celebrate despite the warnings as the beginning of the year surfaced, facing many folks with their private terrors. Like the world would end because a new century began. Hell, Blue told the chestnut colt, who seemed interested finally in listening to what Blue said. Numbers and names were human inventions and had nothing to do with the world itself.

The colt pushed at Blue's hand and Blue patted the damp neck, gathered up the long *mecate* and the reins and turned the stirrup, stuck his boot just inside the wood and leather surface, to let the colt know what was coming, all the time talking to the colt as if the youngster understood. First he'd saddled the colt with a heavy stock saddle and worked him from the ground; now Blue was using a light rig, not meant for roping or long hours but easier on the colt's growing frame.

His hand placed on the prominent withers felt the slightest of trembling; Blue stepped once then swung up onto the saddle, letting himself lie across the seat. The colt's ears went back, his head came around to the left and again to the right, where he could sniff Blue's hand and hear that now-familiar voice telling him this having a human leaning on him was the whole point of the day's lesson.

When the colt seemed agreeable to the procedures, Blue slid down, stood quiet, let the colt turn and sniff him again. The trembling slowed, then quit, Blue's hand placed on the dried neck felt only cooling flesh. Eventually the handsome colt took a deep breath and Blue mounted easily, asked the colt to move forward and got only a few awkward strides before the chestnut found his balance and moved into a long swinging walk.

This was what Blue and Con had seen in the colt, an inch or two over sixteen hands, too big for a decent cow horse, and lean, with great hindquarters, short cannon bone, slender neck, well-sprung ribs. Alert, steady on his feet, the colt always outran the older, bigger colts, even those two years ahead of him. Humans might frighten the chestnut colt but racing and winning, even in the sandy hills and gullied plains, was bred deep.

Blue motioned to one of the now-quiet onlookers to open the gate to the corral, and it was that man Rhynes, a face he thought he knew but didn't bother to ask, a new hire who slid down and did as Blue directed. Blue nodded as he rode through the wide opening, wondering if the man had sense enough to let the colt get a good distance before shutting the gate.

Horse and rider were halfway to the ranch house before Rhynes let the gate swing closed and he jammed down the heavy latch. The colt barely flicked an ear back and Rhynes found he had to admire the man, taking a frantic colt that ran over the boss and Mitchell rode it after a few minutes of what looked like nothing but talking to the animal.

He remembered Mitchell all too well from the Fort, and he remembered the bay gelding Davenport had talked Rhynes and that other fool into overfeeding. Their shenanigans won them the race and their bets, but they took a young man's life in the doing and Rhynes found he didn't have the stomach for cheating. He didn't tell on Davenport, and Sutter never knew why he'd won the race instead of the cowboy or that new lieutenant on the hard-tempered bay.

He sure as hell hadn't expected to find Mitchell here when he rode in asking for work. Word was Mitchell never stayed to one place for long. Rhynes figured, after he'd gotten himself thrown out of the cavalry, that any ranch would do for a home. He'd never cowboyed before, coming into the cavalry from a big city, but he rode well enough now that a ranch raising horses might find him useful.

Norris had the reputation for good horses and fair pay if a man did his work. It'd been pure luck that there was a place for him. Norris didn't even ask for a last name. Just shook his hand and said if he, Rhynes, did his job then he'd be treated fair. Hell of a lot better than the Army was Rhynes' thought as he looked at the old man hiring him. Connor Norris would have cut a fine figure in his day.

There were two other riders here Rhynes remembered. He had never known their names, and when they met up with him at the bunkhouse, nothing showed in their faces 'cepting some sort of welcome, a 'howdy' before they turned away to tend their own business. This being a fair-to-middling cowboy had its advantages.

He knew now they were called Right and Haney. What the hell, a man could choose any name; Rhynes often wished he'd changed his, never did like being called Rhynes even if it was after his granddaddy fought in that damned war.

Rhynes scratched his whiskers, thought about shaving, something he did now only when the mood took him. That Mitchell, he rode the colt up the short hill to the ranch house, right close to a window pulled open, white cloth blowing through, the remains of Norris's woman and her tries to civilize the place before she ran back home to her mama in one of the Carolinas. That's what the bunkhouse gossip said. No one knew when the woman left but the white cloth on those windows looked damned gray and frayed 'round the considerable edges.

The colt stopped at the odd flapping, making enough noise snorting and blowing that the boys watching the peculiar doings could hear and figure that the colt would come unstuck any time now.

Voices, a head stuck out the window, a man's laughter and still the colt was motionless. The only movement up there was Mitchell's hand touching the colt's neck in front of the saddle and the colt's ears flying back and forward. Then it was Norris's laugh, floating down past the corral fence, getting the men smiling on their own. He was a damned fool, that Mitchell, taking one hell of a risk.

Eventually the colt even stuck his head in the window and came back out with cloth in his mouth. Rhynes had to laugh, so did the other men watching the performance. Then it was done.

Rhynes was still grinning when the man turned that colt and came down from the house, hit out across the flat yard to make a circle and come toward the pen. Rhynes guessed, watched the timing and opened the gate just before Mitchell nodded. Horse and rider walked through the opening, then Mitchell guided the colt around the fence, halted while the gate was closed, then did stops and turns and even got a few steps back.

"That's enough." The man's voice was rough, the hands leaning on the saddle horn were heavily scarred and probably told as much about the man's life as Rhynes would ever know. He had found Mitchell to be silent, and the bunkhouse boys told him not to bother, that Norris let Mitchell have his own way. The son of a bitch did a job no one else could. That's all that mattered.

Mitchell stepped down from the offside of the colt, who moved forward quickly, then turned to sniff this strange being in the wrong place.

Mitchell laughed, crossed in front of the colt to strip off the gear and sling it high on the fence before he let the colt go. Mitchell walked to the gate and the colt followed him; Mitchell let the colt catch up, then rubbed his back where the saddle left its mark, until the colt lifted his head and twitched his lip. Rhynes held open the gate again, nodded as Mitchell passed. He found the courage to speak up, something he had to do face to face with the man, the wildness in his eyes a clear warning. Rhynes cleared his throat, spat; "I ain't seen a horse rode that way before."

Mitchell rubbed his jaw; "Any horse makes a better working partner if he ain't scared." Then Mitchell walked on, head tilted, looking back once. Maybe remembering what Rhynes didn't want remembered so Rhynes vowed to keep silent and away from the man. He had a clear vision of that temper when the boy died, it took three troopers to pull Mitchell off Sutter and the sergeant hadn't even been guilty.

He'd hate to have Mitchell figure out his part in the killing accident. It wasn't a real accident; he just didn't know what else to call the boy's death outside of murder. They'd only wanted to slow the horse, nothing more than that. The race brought in some pretty winnings; money Rhynes sent to the boy's father and got back a shaky note of thanks, then he heard two weeks later the old man had died. It was like getting a letter from a ghost.

The incident killed something in Rhynes; the boy's death, then his old man dying. Death drove him from the safety of the cavalry to find out what he was.

TWO

The doc in Valentine sent a woman out to care for Con. It took more'n a week the doc said, to find a woman strong enough to live in Con's house and not take his irritable nature to heart. She had to be mentally secure, so Con figured she'd be ugly and stout, which would be the best thing 'cause a pretty woman would mock Con and upset the boys.

She must have come in on horseback or he would have heard the wagon; squeaky wheels and a lady's team made a lot of noise. Lying in bed, angry and bored, hurting enough to not sleep, Con listened and tried to figure what the boys were doing. Had to have gone to sleep 'cause he never heard a horse enter the yard. He'd been sleeping a lot since the colt ran over him; guess his old bones couldn't deal with breaking and then beginning to heal.

Right Taylor was the foreman now. He might be young for the job but a good man. Right didn't give out favors, not even to his riding buddy Haney, who hadn't changed, who did his work in silence, and scowled, made no friends, kept himself apart from Mitchell especially. Those two sure didn't see eye to eye on much. Con didn't care, the three of them were solid.

She walked into his room without knocking, scared the hell out of Con and he flinched, much as a man can move with a busted wrist and ankle, as she stood looking at him. "Well you're a bundle of nerves aren't you, Mr. Norris." He didn't ask, already knew, but she made the introductions anyway "Yes I'm from Dr. Swann, and my name is Leandra Harpswell." She left Con a pause where a gentleman, at least a man not flat on his backside and beginning to stink from his own flesh and a fever that come up with the broke ankle, a true gentleman would speak his name and say 'how do' or some such nicety and she'd blush lightly and turn her head to avoid looking at him.

Hell with it, Con thought. "There ain't much to you is there. How're you going to lift or care for me, you ain't got the strength, girl. What the hell was the doc thinking?" Damn but she was in a skirt thing, a divided riding skirt current fashion called it, so she rode in, and that made her an independent sort. Con wasn't sure he liked her.

"Mostly, Mr. Norris, I will depend on the fact that you have any number of ranch hands who can use their strength when I tell them what needs to be done. I can wash, and change bandages and cook decent meals and for that one skill alone your men will do as I ask without any hesitation." Goddamn, he thought, she's educated and speaks her mind. Goddamn that doc in Valentine.

He raised his head some, she slid in a pillow and he found it comfortable but by god he wasn't going to tell her. She was not much over five feet and scrawny for his tastes, light through the bosom, sweet waist but hardly any hips at all. Be hard taking hold, nothing to grab on to when a man got rowdy. Then he blushed, felt heat in his face; she wasn't here for such shenanigans but to nurse him back to whatever goddamn health he had left.

Red hair, he liked that; freckles across her nose and on her hands, hair pulled back in that knot women seemed to like. Now Con, he'd want her hair long and flowing and wondered if it was curly but his wife told him loose hair got in the food and caught on drawers and windows and whipped into her mouth from the Nebraska winds so she tied it up and only as a favor to him come nightfall and they was together in their marriage bed would she allow him to unbraid her hair and let it sweep over him.

Hell of a memory for an old man stuck in bed to remember; it gave a man ideas no matter how decrepit he was.

There were bits of light red hairs curled at this girl's forehead and at the base of her neck. It would be beautiful hair left long. And her face, plain, not severe but stern; that face on such a young woman must come from nursing old grouches like him. Light blue eyes that were judging him as he glared at her and made him look away. He hated thinking on what she saw.

Mr. Norris was going to be easy; Leandra had worked as a nurse long enough now to read the signs. He might be a gruff man used to his own way, helpless physically, still angry that his wife left him 'cause he was a tyrant and she let him run over her. Dr. Swann had given her bits of the story so she would be well-warned.

Leandra's education had been in a city, an actual school where they were taught how to deal with men like Connor Norris. Hard men who'd worked their whole life and had little temper to deal with a woman telling them what they had to do.

The Farrand Training School, where she had studied and which was part of Harper Hospital in Detroit, taught their graduates quite well. And the most important aspect of their training was consideration for the patient. Keeping Mr. Norris comfortable while enduring his temper would indeed be a challenge, and Leandra prided herself on rising to meet and conquer all such challenges. Just wait until she gave him a bed bath, and it best be soon for he and the bed on which he was lying smelled much like a pig wallow.

Leandra smiled briefly; "That's settled, Mr. Norris, and no I won't call you Con and you must call me Miss Harpswell. First I will clean up the kitchen, I take it one of the hands came up and provided you with some sort of nourishment, but the mess – it's what a man leaves behind while cooking a simple meal. Lazy, all of you." She cocked her head and let the smallest of smiles lift the corners of her mouth. "I will do the cooking now, for the men as well as you. Whoever has been designated cook needs to rethink his vocation."

With that speech, a lot of which made no sense to Con, the petite Miss Harpswell exited his room and left him lying on the extra pillow, finally able to see outside the window. Damn fool thing, Mitchell riding a half-wild colt on his first saddling up to yell at Con and they both were startled when the colt first looked at the shredded curtains, then reached in and bit and pulled one through the window. Mitchell laughed, so did Con; the colt looked foolish with the corner bit of lace hanging from his mouth.

It was why he gave Blue a full measure of whatever he chose to do; the man had sure instincts about each horse and they mostly came out right. Good man to have on a ranch that raised a lot of its own stock. Or bought from neighbors, unbroken colts that Con preferred, now that he had Blue Mitchell. . .Con rolled his head until the extra pillow got flattened perfect, then he closed his eyes and slept.

First thing was to put her valise in the small room off the kitchen that had obviously been the departed wife's sewing room. It was small, had a nice bed in it, a table and chair, good light from two windows, and close to the outside facilities. The poor woman must have escaped Con Norris's temper and advances and come here to do her woman's work safely surrounded by a good sewing kit and crochet needles, with balls of yarn left behind to gather dust. Materials were stacked high, mostly sprigged florals meant to be dresses that were never made.

Leandra would tend to the kitchen after taking care of her horse. She could, of course, ask one of the men lazing around the corrals to do this chore, but she was both particular about her gray horse's care, and did not wish the men to presume she was dependent upon their services.

She had grown used to taking care of her life, and that included the necessity of leading Tennyson to a smaller corral that was empty, and tying him inside while she undid the latigo, threaded it through the cinch ring so she wouldn't step on the length of leather, went around and hung the cinch on a special tab, and pull off the heavy saddle. Despite it being built for her mother, it weighed a good thirty pounds and was an effort for Leandra to handle. The no-goods sitting on the fence watched her struggle, but fortunately they made no unseemly comments or so much as considered flirting with her. Silent watching she could handle.

Then a lean man came from a small barn, carefully pulling the door latch shut. He walked toward her and she was startled by his appearance.

This was no ordinary ranch hand or cowboy. In some undefined manner he was quite unique. He was studying her as he approached, face calm, an easy swing to his movements that told her he rode a great deal. But he moved differently than most bowlegged cowhands.

There was a slight limp, and one arm hung crookedly; a horse breaker no doubt, one of those who terrified their mounts into submission, hence the accumulation of scars and badly-set bones. She offered him the slightest of smiles; he stopped and smiled back and she found his face and manner quite extraordinary.

It was the eyes at first, startlingly blue, a shade she had not encountered before; almost the exact color of the native stones. The man nodded to her, then quickly looked away, as if something terrible might come from staring.

His hair was long, lightly curled over his shirt collar, and of a graying blond that was attractive. In his parts he was not handsome, with a long face and several scars across his right brow, but all together, in his height, the easy grace, and those amazing eyes, he became more and more intriguing. His voice startled her; it was low-pitched and well-modulated, each word spoken clearly. And there was no antagonism in his tone, a simple quiet voice that made her feel comfortable. And that in turn made Leandra uneasy, for she was used to suspecting men of their intentions, and certainly not being comforted by any of them.

"Ma'am, you leave your gear to the fence, why then some small critter'll have it chewed in no time." Without waiting, Blue walked past her and picked up the saddle and bridle, wondering at its lightness. He carried the saddle in one hand, grasped the bridle and blanket in the other, and when he reached the saddle-house door, he balanced the saddle on his knee and lifted the hand-made thumb latch.

She followed him inside, and without turning to check on her, he laid the saddle upended on the pommel, kept the bridle in his hand as he reached up to move Norris's old saddle to a higher rung. The working saddles sat end-to-end on a long barrel on legs, with Con's gear at the front.

"Ma'am, we'll put your rig here for the time. Con ain't, ah, won't have use for it for some months or so." Sliding her saddle onto the barrel, he smoothed out the blanket over the seat, wet side up to dry easily, and hung the bridle from the horn. "Nice rig, ma'am." Blue thought a moment, he didn't want to be forward or nosey; "Where'd you get a Heiser made for a lady?"

Leandra had been asked many different questions, most of them rude, about her life, why she was who she was, why wasn't she married, didn't she find all this nursing work difficult for a sensitive and petite lady. But no one ever asked about the saddle. She snorted, a most unladylike response; the man grinned and she liked him even more.

"It was made for my mother." There, let him swallow that story and see what he thought. "She would have been quite a woman, not riding side-saddle. You've taken a lot from her."

It was not a conversation she expected at an all-male ranch. More often it was derision and disbelief, not acceptance and a kindly humor. This was a man to avoid, as were all cow hands and especially those who broke the horses. And it was easy to see which branch of the rancher species this man belonged in.

"Ma'am, I'll see that your gray gets water and feed. I think the foreman rode in just now for the men are getting busy at their chores. You might want to make his acquaintance. He deals with Con on most matters. I sure ain't the one who gives the orders."

She thought of many answers and comments and the only thing her mouth would open and say was; "His name is Tennyson." That indeed made the man grin, and those remarkable eyes sparked.

"My horse's name." She was shamed, almost girlish in her blushing as she pushed herself past him to meet the rest of the Norris crew. He spoke over her head; "Yes, ma'am, I read some of his stuff. Writes pretty good for a horse, don't he." The words followed her and she was startled by them. Swann had told her in detail about Connor Norris, his long-escaped wife, the peculiar assortment of men working for him. But he had assured her they were range-taught gentlemen and would be nothing but polite to her, that was the only kind of hands Mr. Norris kept to his place.

This one, with the turquoise eyes and sense of humor, and good manners when he thought to remember, she already knew he was going to be trouble.

THREE

Being foreman hadn't been what he expected. Right Taylor lived loose and free for most of his working years and he liked the independence. When Con asked him to stay on, it took some thinking, and even a few questions to Blue on the matter.

Blue Mitchell. That was one hard man, to ride with and to know. He came in the last time sore, bent, too goddamn quiet. Right knew why, didn't have to ask. He'd been there for the race, had been witness to Mitchell's fury when the boy died.

As the new foreman, he didn't make a fuss about that extra bay gelding with the fresh USA brand and a signed paper from one Colonel Radcliff giving ownership to Blue; it was the man himself got to Right. He'd rode with him, been through some hell, come back mostly in one piece but this time it was all different.

Even Con Norris could read the man's sorrow and sent Blue and a few young colts up to a line camp for winter work. Grub once a week, lots of long fence to ride, miles on the colts, time for Blue to heal. Like when he rode in that first time maybe seven years ago, with the lamed brown and a half-broke dun colt. Con had known the name, let Mitchell stay without putting him right to work. Give the man time, Con said. A Blue Mitchell-trained horse had a higher value, made a better working mount. Con had never met the man but the reputation was steady and came from reliable neighbors. Right almost asked how Con knew the man was Mitchell, until he saw the face and those eyes, and was reminded the gent's name was Blue. His folks sure 'nough had a good reason for the naming.

Right packed the supply sack with a bottle of whiskey first trip to the cabin this time, even though Blue didn't have much use for drink, and when it was gone the second week, he kept putting in a fresh-filled bottle, never saying nothing, never letting himself notice the blood-shot eyes, the greasy hair and rank smell.

About the third month, after Right had spoke about Christmas and did he want coming in, Blue showed him a half-full whiskey bottle and said it was enough to last the rest of the winter. Said no to Christmas, as Right expected, but it was a kindness to let the man know he had a place if he wanted.

That spring the chestnut colt was a yearling and already it was evident the colt was different from the regular ranch stock. His mama was a decent-bred mare from the mid-west, and the papa was a race-winning sire put to stud for the Army program. Those men with the dollars, they wanted papers, proof so the horse could run on the fancy tracks and win the high-stakes purses.

Right knew about bush racing. He'd gone along with Blue a few times, marveled at what the man could get out of an ordinary horse, setting on that rolled-up blanket he used as a saddle, said he learned it from the Indians, lost too many races to them while he rode upright in a stock saddle.

Now Con was talking 'bout running the chestnut, or selling him. After Con's wreck, while they was carrying him up to the ranch house, he give out the word that Blue was to work the colt and no one else was to touch him, go near him, spook him or do anything against what Blue said. Rhynes learned his lesson, so did the other one, Blake. They'd felt the edge of Blue's temper, then Right had done the explaining all over again, especially to Skippy, who started out listening to the lecture whining and rubbing his butt.

When Right got to the end of his talk, Skippy quit rubbing at his backside and walked off without a word.

Right almost recognized Rhynes in the beginning; the face had a familiar set but so many of the drifters come through had that same hard-luck stare so he put off fretting over who the man was until after the dust-up with Blue and the colt, and then the man made his confession. He'd been part of the death race to Fort Robinson that time. He didn't much want Blue to know, Rhynes told him. He was doing his penance, wanted to start a clean life, had come to respect Blue and his actions at the Fort, and wanted in turn to earn the man's respect.

Right had to do some serious thinking on the notion of repentance and a new start. He said later he guessed it was all right with him, but if Blue figured it out, or knew that Right had known, god it was complicated and all Right wanted to do was run the ranch with Norris laid up in bed. But if any of this came out, it was for Rhynes to explain. Right had too much else to do, mostly confined to getting the men at their chores without none of them quitting on him.

That woman up to the house scared Right; she looked into him and shook her head and told him he had to send two men up on a regular basis, morning, noon and evening, for the heavy lifting and personal attentions their boss needed and she would accept no excuse.

In turn she would cook decent meals, and perhaps teach whoever had taken on the job how to prepare and present food in a manner far more pleasing than slopped beans burned at the edges, biscuits you could play baseball with and jams so sour that a toothless man's mouth would collapse.

All that talk and telling him and Right could think only on the color of her hair and that she would be the boss of him and the boys for a month or so. She seemed to him a combination of hell and his church-fearing mama.

She was pretty though, Miss Leandra who told him to call her Miss Harpswell but the name didn't fit and he got stubborn about it so she finally nodded at the end of their contentious conversations and said that 'Miss Leandra' would do, from him only.

He was feeling pretty good until she added one last detail; "Especially don't let that man with the blue eyes use my given name. He is quite intimidating." Her voice trailed off and Right knew that Blue Mitchell already made himself a conquest and once he again he'd done it without trying. There were times in Right's sorry life he could hate a man based only on what he hadn't done, and at this point, with the lady looking moony-eyed at Blue, he could strangle the man for what he was on looks, nothing to do with who he'd shown himself to be.

Right noticed all the preparations the woman had made to the supper meal; she put out the food in white bowls, with a spoon in each dish; potatoes, some vegetable, slabs of meat on a plate with a fork stuck in the middle, damned good gravy in a strange-looking pitcher she said he could pour from, not have to ladle or make a mess. He nodded to her and she turned her back, asked Blue in a softened voice if he too wanted gravy.

Right grinned across the table; "Hell, Blue, don't scare this one off, she cooks too good." It was all he could do to remain civil, but he knew, it was his own jealousy over a sweet-looking woman didn't think much of him. What he thought of when he saw Miss Leandra wasn't the usual bedroom activities and even that thought entering his head made him blush.

It was good enough the boys were taken up with her cooking and not paying to attention to Right and his peculiar thoughts.

Blue shrugged off Right's comment; "Ain't no biscuits." Right shook his head and kept eating. Food didn't matter much to Blue, he was more'n likely thinking 'bout the chestnut and riding him again, getting some miles and fitness on the colt. Now Right, he appreciated a tender steak, good fried potatoes, and hot biscuits, 'specially with honey or sorghum. Damn Mitchell for pointing out a particular failing. Far as Right could see, this woman had her no faults at all. Even her commands and decision sounded like private music.

The next morning Blue had the colt caught and saddled before breakfast. Right stood at the saddle-house door and watched as his old riding buddy seemed to smooth the colt's hide, turn the head and neck to each side, drawing his hands down the neck, stroking the shoulders, then tightening the cinch and stepping aboard in an easy motion that gave the colt nothing to fear. The youngster started out with a sorry lurch, then walked off like it was his tenth year of being ridden. The man was good.

Miss Leandra reminded Right that she needed a team of men up to the house. He volunteered himself and Haney, a surly son of a gun but another one Right trusted. One of the few in his sorry life. At least the women didn't take to Haney like they did with Mitchell.

It wasn't much this time, just getting Mr. Norris set in a chair, looking out the window to his land, his corrals and horses. Con growled about the men not doing their work and Right told him of Blue already out on the chestnut, Rhynes and Blake riding fence to the Sidwell homestead pasture and why Right and Haney, they was doing their house chores like they was supposed to do. Skippy'd been sent to a dry well to see if he could dig out a few feet of silt and find water again. That Skippy didn't like the chore, Right could see it in his eyes. It was one of the worst jobs on the ranch, as Right and Mitchell both knew.

Right's job wasn't to keep Skippy happy; in fact he was hoping to annoy the son of a bitch so's he'd ride on. There were always hands coming through, riding the grub line. Though in Right's thinking, there were fewer now and most of them were old-timers. He had a feeling that the life he'd always wanted was beginning to disappear.

Con threw a book at Right and the men retreated, Haney grunting some insult and Right as usual laughing. The boss played the grouch, why not let him. Broke wrist, broke ankle; that was enough hell on a strong man who'd done for himself most of his life. Norris had been in that bloody War and never talked of it. Right knew only because he'd found an old wood canteen, with the hand-cut CSA letters on it. Canteen had been hidden far to the back in the saddle-house, behind old harness and useless gear. When Right wetted his thumb and rubbed it across some scratching, he could read a name; C Norris, Co. I Texas Partisan Raiders.

That evening it was some roasted bird and more vegetables, a cherry cobbler and Right thought he would suggest to the boss that the woman needed to stay on after he was healed. Help in the house or something.

When he entered the cook kitchen to thank her, she put her hands on her hips, in fists, and told him straight to his face; "I don't stay on after the patient no longer needs my assistance. I don't cook or clean unless it's an illness, and no I'm not married, and I most certainly don't intend to be." Right retreated without getting in a word but he already knew he was in love.

He found Blue in a corner of the bunkhouse, staring at two thick poles, cut down from a soft willow near the stream. Blue looked up only when Right stood direct in front of him and asked; "What the hell're you thinking on now?"

Blue answered sideways, not unexpected, and Right grinned as he listened. "That chestnut colt's something else, Right. Mr. Norris he got himself a wonder. That man was here, he's going to buy the colt for someone I bet, and I envy him. Hell of a colt. I rode up into the draws, got onto the mesa and let him out some. He can fly, thought we'd go off the edge in a full run. He don't understand stop or turn yet but my god, Right."

Right laughed, Mitchell always ran true to his passion. "Blue, I asked what you was doing now, with them sticks, not about any ole horse." Blue looked at him, those rare eyes straight on Right and he wanted to take a step back or punch that face. Damn the son but then it wasn't his fault he was born looking like a crazy man.

It took a moment, of Blue staring at the wood in his hands, smoothing one peeled section, then looking back up quickly at Right. The man knew; he'd lived with it his whole life. He must have paid deep with riding by his lonesome.

"I'm carving out crutches, Right. Any decent man needs to get himself around never mind he's got that woman to nurse him. It's too damn painful having a pretty thing like her help a growed man piss or worse."

He could only shake his head; Mitchell would think of the particulars. Then again Right had seen the hole in Mitchell's chest. Had to have been a long time laid flat on a bed, women nursing him; of course he'd know how it felt.

"You keep working on the chestnut, Con says he wants that colt hard and fit and with the best manners. I think he's seeing dollars instead of hide and bone belonging to a three-year-old." Blue's head jerked up and he got his mouth ready to argue, then saw into Right's face, took in the easy smile and looked away, nodding, hands returning to their work on the wood.

Blue knocked at the back door and waited until he heard a yell telling him to 'get in here goddamnit' and knew that the girl was either out of the house or tending to Con. So he did as he was told and sure enough the kitchen was empty and he could hear fussing and low curses from Con's room.

He laid the crutches against the door and entered in time to find the young woman lifting Con's hips onto a white pan and Blue looked away. Con grunted; "You come here, Mitchell. I ain't having this child touch me." Her face turned to him and while her eyes were vivid and filled with anger, her face was white, and he could read the pulse in her neck and knew that Con's temper had dug in.

Blue smiled gently, slid between Miss Harpswell and Con's bed and grinned at the old man. "You hush, Con, and leave her be. She's helping you 'less you want to lie in your own piss, pardon, ma'am. She ain't here to torment you." Con glared at him; "She's young and female and I'm a damn-near useless man three times her age and she ain't touching me there 'less she means it and there ain't no chance in hell of that happening."

Stare to stare, two men seeing the other, a mutual understanding but still the problem wasn't solved. Blue reached under Con's back and lifted him, the woman shoved the pan in and Blue jerked his head, she left the room. Then he raised the edge of Con's gown and left the old man to his noisy relief.

She was in the kitchen when Blue went there to wash up. "Thank you, mister." She'd already forgotten. "Mitchell", he said. "Blue." She nodded absently. "Did I hit a pair of crutches when I was being banished?" She swung around and stared at him. "You made them. Well, they certainly will end the obvious problem we were having."

Blue kept washing, feeling gritty and unclean; "That's their purpose, ma'am." She gave him a towel; he dried off and left without saying nothing more.

It was easier dealing with the colt, who'd gotten familiar enough with Blue and the routine that he tried playing instead of standing to be caught, snorting and running from Blue's approach with the bridle. So Blue kind of twisted the reins and threw them at the colt, kept him trotting around the pen, turning him occasionally by stepping toward his head and throwing the reins again, kept the colt going a good ten minutes until there was an easy rhythm to the colt's long trot and Blue could hear the snorting breath, see the ribs rise and fall. He worked the colt a few more turns of the pen until a shiny dark wet appeared on the neck and at the loins.

Then he stopped and waited and the colt eased in closer, stopped himself, turned and looked at Blue. It was a simple matter to walk up and offer the bit, pull the headstall over the colt's poll, real careful around the twitching ears, setting the leather in place so it didn't pinch at the base of those ears. Blue turned and walked toward his gear, and the colt followed without a tug.

Only then did Blue realize he had Rhynes and that other man standing and watching. Blake, that was his name, shook his head and muttered about a waste of time. Rhynes started to speak then shut his mouth as Blue walked past him.

The colt was sweaty and wanting to rub his face on Blue's arm. Blue shook the colt's head away, tugged lightly on the off rein to straighten the colt's neck and saddled up quick, stepped into the saddle and that Rhynes fellow opened the pen gate, stood back and Blue and the colt blasted out at a good trot, headed for the mesa and a run, some work on turning and stops, now that he had the colt's attention.

He got back mid-afternoon and the place was deserted. Men were out on fence or doctoring cattle, Skippy down in that well, Blake or whatever his name was looking to the spring crop from Con's good mares. They were Con's pleasure and it must be killing the man to lie in that bed, aching on diagonal sides and pissed off at the world closed in around him. The colt's mama, she was expecting another foal by the same sire; Blue knew that Con wished against common sense to repeat what he'd gotten three years ago.

Blue unsaddled the colt, who was sweaty but cool, no heat under the saddle blankets, only dried sweat along his neck and quarters.

"That's hard riding for such a young horse. I am surprised Mr. Norris allows you the leeway to treat a lovely animal like this one in such a manner." Blue kept to his chore, her voice had startled him but the words were expected. She had to be soft-hearted about animals, caring as she did for the sick and dying. Otherwise she'd never survive as a nurse. And she sure wouldn't make much of a rancher's wife.

He scrubbed off the dried sweat, checked the colt's hooves, rubbed those quick-moving ears as he slid off the bridle and the colt stayed still for the rubbing. Letting out a sigh and a fart, content to stand with Blue, until Blue pushed the colt gently on the shoulder and then turned to face the woman.

She glared at him, which was what he'd figured on; then she looked past him to watch the colt walk to a soft spot in the pen, dig, lower himself carefully, front end first, and roll, stand, shake, and come back to Blue for some more rubbing on his ears and at the withers.

"Guess I didn't ride him too hard, ma'am. He kinda likes getting out to run. It's what he's bred for." That might have gone over the unseen line, for her face wasn't pretty right then, tight and thinned. Then unexpectedly she laughed. "You know, Mr. Mitchell, I think I might have misjudged you." Blue stroked the colt's neck; "Ma'am, I try not to judge folks." He gave her a moment, then; "You want, I'll catch up your literary horse and you might get out for a ride. I'll go set with Con, he probably needs a ranch hand to yell at 'bout now."

She wanted to be angry but it simply wasn't possible; he'd called her on a failing she had long ago recognized in herself, then made a generous offer. And yes she was tired of being cooped up in the house. Mr. Norris was a less-than-pleasant patient, as she had been warned, and perhaps taking a short ride would clear her head and give her the strength needed to deal with Norris and his irritable fretting.

"Thank you, Mr. Mitchell." "You're welcome, ma'am." It could be so simple, talk between different people, as long as they knew their manners.

He put his gear in the saddle-house and picked up her saddle, left the blanket and bridle and she accepted this as an invitation to help. She followed him, feeling somewhat like the chestnut colt, appalled and fascinated at the same time, and trusting the man despite his peculiar style.

Tennyson obviously enjoyed being curried and brushed, and Leandra stood at his head, saw the gray's pleasure and allowed herself to relax and enjoy by proxy the care this man put into grooming her horse. She had never considered the horse's part in the process; it was usually a matter of cleaning the back and cinch area to prevent sores. That she understood, having attended lectures on bedsores and how to treat them in patients.

She wasn't paying enough attention when Mitchell asked for the bridle and Leandra realized Tennyson was saddled, waiting, horse and man placid as he held out a hand and she hurriedly dropped the bridle across his palm. He grinned and she felt foolish.

"All ready, ma'am. Have a good ride." He was gone, a lonesome figure walking with an unsteady grace, headed toward the house with its dark interior and unforgiving inhabitant. For now it didn't matter, she had Tennyson and a few hours of freedom.

FOUR

"What the hell you doing here middle of the day?" "Old man you get up out of that stinking bed and use them crutches." "Can't, damnit, got a busted wing."

Blue leaned on the doorframe; "Con, I made a special grip if you'd take time to notice. Up under your arm, with a rest for the broke bone, a wide grip for those fingers sticking out of those wrappings. Hell man, you been in here 'most two weeks now and you're looking like one of them Easterners you laugh at, all flour white and poorly. It ain't fitting for a Nebraska man."

Con's face turned red and his mouth opened, then shut, opened again. Blue pretended he didn't notice. "Here." He walked into the room and handed Con the crudely carved pair of crutches, skinned down like their new owner, pale wood damp to the touch, releasing a pleasing scent from the core that wasn't strong enough to hide Con's stink but was a reminder of soft rains, tree lines, good pasture, a fall storm.

It was in the old man's dark blue eyes, pure fury turned to memory and then he took the one crutch into his good hand, fitted to his upper arm, balanced himself against the ankle break.

They both studied the odd crutch, with a wide, scooped rest for the upper arm and forearm: Blue turned it, placed Con's

34

broke wrist in the support, pushed the contraption up close to the man's body.

"That's your good leg so use it, good arm holds up the bad leg, hell man you can hobble 'round, get yourself to sun and air and maybe sanity. The feeling won't last, but it's a start."

"Mitchell, you're fired." Blue straightened, looked at the old man facing him. Face full of white whiskers, something spotted on his chin, more dribbles of food down his nightshirt. Fingers showing swollen and too white through the dirty covering on the broke wrist, the ankle no better. "You fire me, Con, who'll ride that colt? I saw his mama this morning, she's got a nice filly to her side. Not going to be as big as this colt but she'll make one hell of a broodmare. Built for speed just like you wanted." He watched the facts sink in; "Like that fella wants to buy from you, comes all the way here to see the colt and you had to show off and doing so put you in this bed."

He waited that moment, a small time when choices are made and can't be taken back. Then he turned, got to the door and heard Con's voice; "Blue, you keep riding that damned colt. I ain't that much a fool" Then another time of silence and hesitation and Blue forced himself to breathe in and out, knowing how his own tightness affected the colt. "Thanks." Con's voice quivered but the word was real. Blue nodded without turning around.

Blue saddled one of Con's favorite, a bay roan gelding the boss called Sully, with quick feet and too damned smart but the roan listened to Con, and would work for Blue under a light hand. He slipped a simple bit into the roan's mouth, the horse naturally tried to bite him and that made Blue laugh.

He figured to keep some condition on the roan, lower the heat of his temper, and check on the broodmare band at the same time. He needed to see it again, that pretty filly standing next to her mama, those long clean legs still shaky from birth. There was another mare carrying a late foal by the same

Thoroughbred sire as Curly; Blue wanted to check on her, hated thinking that something might go wrong.

The roan fought back with half-bucks and sideways two-steps when Blue held the reins close. Eventually the gelding settled into his best gait, a long-striding trot that shook an old man's insides less he stood and held to the saddle swell and let his ankles and knees take the beating instead of his ass and innards.

When he got to the mares, the roan stood and whinnied and the mares barely looked up. The newborns' cries were high and shrill, a sound that let Blue set back and smile. "They are quite sweet, aren't they Mr. Mitchell." He jumped sideways in the saddle, the roan bogged his head and got in a few good bucks before Blue spurred him forward and hauled up his head so the roan ended up turning too fast to the right and almost fell over himself.

"Well that was more than I expected." It was the nurse of course, on her pretty gray with the black legs and tail. Blue wiped his mouth, tasting grit; "Ma'am, it ain't right smart to ride up on a man thinking. Hard as it is to think, you might could scare him and his horse to boot."

She looked confused, then thoughtful, until finally she laughed. "You are always a surprise." He touched the roan's neck, let out a breath; "Don't mean to be, ma'am. Just how I see things I guess."

Thankfully she had the sense to be quiet while she looked down into the small valley where the mares grazed. Blue's heart returned to a decent rhythm and he spoke without looking at the woman. "It's special to watch the foals, they got so much ahead of them. Some'll be good working horses, others'll buck naturally, like this roan here. I think Con keeps him because he can ride him while the horse's thrown most of the hands."

Then it occurred to him he was talking on too much. The silence was a shock, her gray turned restless and the roan laid back his ears in warning. Blue left it for the woman to do the talking. That was how he understood things got run in this world. She surprised him.

"Humans are the same, Mr. Mitchell. There is so much potential in each of us as children and so few actually reach their dreams. They need the correct guidance also in order to get there. Training if you will." The words went in deep and hard and he flinched as if stabbed. Leandra watched the transformation, saw the mouth tighten, the eyes go dark and his hands clenched on the reins so the roan threw his head, then half-reared.

He was gentleman enough to recognize his reaction was disproportionate to her idle comments. "Sorry, ma'am, you caught me off guard again." She wanted to ask from what, talking about horses to a man who trained them for a living? And then connecting their training to the human condition. This was indeed a most peculiar cowhand.

It was the roan moving restlessly that told her; "I have a few more miles to put on him 'fore I'm done, nice talking with you. Ma'am." His voice had slowed, returned to its easy drawl that said little about his thoughts or sensibilities. She had the notion she'd never see that startled and distressed face again.

She rode in early, slightly tired from the distance she and Tennyson had traveled. As she unsaddled, she found herself wishing for the horseman who so easily lifted her saddle onto the rack inside the saddle-house. She struggled and was done with the chore, dusty and exhausted, when one of the hands, a man introduced earlier as Haney, walked in, grunted at her and swung his rig up onto the barrel if it were simply a blanket and perhaps a bridle without its bit. She hated men at that moment, their casual strength and lack of manners. He barely looked at her, grunted again as he disappeared out the door. She would have yelled at him but her mouth was dry and unexpectedly she wanted to weep.

Of all things, Mr. Norris was standing outside, long nightshirt flapping but his arms rested on the crude crutches Mr. Mitchell had fashioned. He bellowed at her as she climbed the shallow hill. "Beautiful day, girl. Can't wait for supper." Before she could correct him, he turned and swung himself across the porch and into the house. It was already happening, these arrogant men were taking her presence for granted.

It occurred to her that supper could be cold meat and the canned beets she knew they disliked, but then Mr. Norris was sitting in his chair, bare ankles protruding, eyelids slowly closing, and she could hear tired voices outside, the sounds of men who'd worked all day. Punishing them for her turmoil seemed cruel and certainly not in keeping with her chosen work.

After supper, stranded in the hot kitchen washing and drying and knowing she needed to tend Mr. Norris, she was herself surprised. That voice, low and soft, gentle and intended not to spook her. "Ma'am." Said from the back door, out in the cool air while she suffocated inside with the cook stove and hot water.

"Ma'am. I want to 'pologise for talking harsh to you today." It was Mr. Mitchell, holding a few wilting flowers in one big hand. She smiled; "You're just the person I wanted to see. Those crutches work well, but Mr. Norris is tired now, would you help him get into bed? I'll come tend to him later."

Mitchell laid the flowers down near the sink and walked toward the old man's bedroom. He was easy this time, no fire in those eyes, nothing tight or scared in him. She still wondered what her few innocent words spoken earlier had set off inside the cowboy's mind.

"Con, here, let me get you up and don't give me no trouble." He held gently to the trembling arm and Con actually smiled at him while they staggered to the bed. "She's a pretty one for sure, Blue. Don't blame you." Blue let the old man set, then laid him out on the bed. "Con, don't go reading nothing you don't understand. She ain't for me, I don't trust good women and if they're smart they know it and stay away."

He left by Con's own back door, not heading through the kitchen, no more shared words or laughter with the woman, no more of this foolishness. He caught up a rank three-year-old and slipped on a bosal, his old saddle, and let the colt run straight at the hills and the distant mesa, into the night's darkness that might hide his thoughts.

That first day Con appeared out of the house fully dressed and held up by those pealed wood crutches, the corral was empty, the men out at work.

With him was the wide-set man who'd been there the day Con got trampled. He spoke quickly to Con in a harsh voice that carried. Blue had the colt halfway out to the hills and drew him up, did an easy turn over the hocks and let the colt trot back to the corrals.

There was a look to Con, a half-smile on the worn face that could be read as gratitude. "Morning, Blue. This here's Ores Trefethern. He's come to. . ." The words died and Blue nodded; "I remember you from that day." The man nodded with a grunt. Blue went on; "You've come back to see how the colt's doing." Again that nod accompanied by a louder grunt.

There was a flat stretch of beaten grass before trails separated to different sections of the ranch. Blue inclined his head, Con grinned. The colt resisted going away from the corrals until Blue bent the colt's neck, using the light bit soft in the young mouth, pushed against his side with a leg and the colt unstuck himself, went into that easy trot as Blue lined him up to the far end of the flat.

Con raised and dropped his hand, grabbing quickly for the slipping crutch. Trefethern made no attempt to help; he was watching the chestnut colt while holding a ticking watch spread across his thick hand.

Despite the saddle horn and swell, the heavy weight and Blue's size, the colt bolted when Blue signaled by leaning forward, heels pressed to the colt's sides. It was a huge spring to a gallop that quickly flattened into pure speed. Blue was laughing, hands soft on the reins, feeling the colt's mouth, telling him to run.

He raised his eyes briefly, to look sideways and see the startled faces of the two men. He risked taking one hand off the reins to give a salute, then took back the soft leather, steadied the colt and asked for that last burst of speed.

When it was time, he drew the colt up, resisting the shaking head, the harsh pull on the bit; telling the colt no, listen, come slower, trot now, walk easy. In a circle that widened to take horse and rider back to the men, the horse dancing sideways, Blue loose in the saddle, hands gentle and insisting on the reins; listen, come back, it's done.

The colt kept shaking his head against Blue's command through the reins, until finally the chestnut came to a stop and Blue dropped the reins, patted the sweaty neck and the colt stretched his head almost to the ground.

Trefethern looked at his watch; Con nodded to the man.

It was three days later than Con Norris made it to the corrals again, fully dressed 'cepting for the bound ankle and the bum wrist that was wadded in stiffened cloth so he gimped along on the crutches and scared the hell out of the boys getting used to no boss telling them what to do. They listened some to Right but without the threat of Con's presence it was getting rough moving Blake and Skippy to their chores. Rhynes surprised Right, and Con, out riding fence without complaint, doctoring a few pink-eyed calves and Haney, now, he was never different, grumbling and working hard and arguing with Blue over horses and such.

Right found he was glad to see the boss come down and the men hopped off that fence and looked busy catching up their best horses and readying to ride. Blue had that chestnut colt in the large corral and the big youngster was riding smooth, turning quick, coming to a sweet halt.

Even Right was impressed and he'd known Blue a few years now. The colt was toughened, leaned down and fit and full of himself, entire and finding out about fillies and those scents coming to him on the air. Yet Blue kept the youngster mannerly enough to be ridden, but there were times Right was glad he wasn't in that saddle. No sir.

Con was watching him. Flat eyes staring, head lowered, like a goddamn bull Blue thought. Readying for a fight. Damn, wonder what he'd done this time. But if Con pushed him on the colt, he'd push back, there was no way Blue would ruin a colt this good. That show-off run in front of the stocky man had taken a lot out of the colt. Blue was rebuilding the colt's strength with long slow trots, a few easy gallops, time in the corral learning better manners.

He put the colt through his paces, making a few fancy turns and stops, a steady backing. Then he rode up to where Con was resting on those spindly crutches and Blue halted the colt, doubled his hands on the saddle horn and waited. Then said; "What, old man?" He'd lost patience with the whole goddamn game. Silence usually didn't bother Blue but this time, with that old man staring at him, he was getting restless.

It figured with Blue's insult that Con would lose his temper but the sweetest big smile crossed the man's face and filled out most of the wrinkles and that got Blue to laugh at his own foolish posturing.

"What, Con? Tell us 'fore Haney there blows a hole in his head scratching and trying to figure." Haney turned to look at Blue and barely grunted; "Don't care, Mitchell, and you know it." Blue leaned over and patted the colt's drying neck. "Haney, sometimes you're just too damned easy."

"I sold the colt for ten thousand dollars. Thought you yahoos might want to know that." Con's voice had a fine hint of laughter in it. Even the colt stood quiet, all the men froze in their tracks. Ten thousand dollars, a man could live a whole life on that much. Blue found his voice first; "Who. . .where?"

"To New York, Mitchell. Some place called Brighton Beach on a goddamn island." Blue rubbed his face, fingers dug hard into his eyes. "What?" The colt shifted under him and Blue wanted to get off, dismount, hand the reins to Con or Right or anyone else. Ten thousand dollars and he was setting on it.

"New York. The train goes direct to the racetrack. And you're going with him, Blue. He's insured but the man wants his trainer making the trip and I said yes since he promised to pay out your expenses with a bonus. You're traveling in a private car on the railroad with the colt."

Slowly the gathered men were beginning to make noises, some even breathing again, a few kicking at the dirt, one, Right Taylor, actually touched the colt's shoulder. Right's voice was rough but he seemed to find words for all the silent hands as he spoke to the chestnut colt; "Son, you got a hell of a surprise coming." Blue figured the words applied to him as well.

FIVE

Blue unsaddled the colt, saw his hands tremble as he slid off the bridle. He took his time, didn't turn to Con or the other men, who were staring at him or more likely at the chestnut colt. None of them had seen a horse worth that much money. Blue wanted to yell at Con so he forced himself to wait while his gut settled and he could see past the immediate and unforgiving terror. The East coast; New York City.

He left the colt in the corral, fresh hay, good water, a rubdown and a check on each leg, no swelling, no splints or knots; tendons hard, knees cool. Blue stood, pushed his hands against his back. The men were finally gone, Con had limped back to the house, Haney reluctantly beside the boss, not holding but going along just in case.

Still restless, gut really hurting now, Blue turned back to the horse trap to see who'd come up for water. A big red roan belonging to Haney, a four-year-old ridden hard today by Rhynes, and a sour-mouthed buckskin Con kept saying he was going to sell. The buckskin would do for what Blue needed.

He shut the gate on the water trap, let the horses run a bit then settle, and roped out the buckskin. The hot-tempered horse fought him, and Blue fought back, struggling with his temper, the edge he felt pushing him. The buckskin snorted and turned, stared down the rope at Blue and he let it rest, giving some on the tight line, talking out loud to the horse and hearing his own words.

"S'all right, son, easy, settle down now. New York ain't that scary. She's nearby I think. But I ain't going looking for her, not at all. See, you got no need to get upset, me either, it's just a trip with a horse and back here, maybe some extra money put in a bank. Doing something I've never done, seeing places I've only read about. I'm getting too old you know, it sure wouldn't hurt if I put by some cash." Blue noted that his thoughts were confused, between the pretty nurse and going East thinking of another woman. Hell of a mess for a cowboy to be caught in.

The buckskin snorted and Blue accepted that as animal agreement. He hauled the horse to the tie rail near the saddle-house and got out his gear. As he mounted and turned the buckskin loose, headed to the hills, he heard a small voice call his name, and he put spurs to the horse, got a high buck and some speed in return.

"Mr. Taylor." "Right, ma'am. I know it's peculiar but it's what my pa called me." His hands were wet and the supper lay in his belly like lead stones, god she was a pretty little thing.

"Mr. Taylor." She was stubborn too, he admired that in a person. "What took Mr. Mitchell away from supper? Is there something wrong?" Of course it was about Blue, damn that one for his ways.

"Ma'am, he gets moody and catches up a rough horse. They kind of fight it out and Blue's some better for a day or two. He don't never hurt them none, he only takes out a bad 'un can use the riding. Sometimes he comes back scratched or lamed but it don't last. And he don't never hurt the horse."

She smiled at him, rested one small hand on his arm and his heart quit. "Mr. Taylor, please call me Miss Leandra." He would oblige but his mouth went dry and any words or thoughts dried up too. Finally, though, his heart got thumping again proper.

Right shook his head, swallowed hard; "Ma'am, there ain't no use worrying about Blue. He's got his own world, and the rest of us ain't invited in. Something's got to him, mostly about that colt I figure, and he'll ride it out, come back quiet and it's best to leave him alone then." More words than he thought were in him but there was a strong need to protect Blue.

"Mr. Taylor. . .ah, Right, you seem to know Mr. Mitchell well." He nodded, stunned at the length of his own speechifying and her continued questions. "Yes, ma'am, Miss Leandra. I rode with him some over the years."

"Do you trust him, Mr. Taylor?" She wasn't going to give in easily as he did. "Ma'am, I've seen him ride, been with him when he held a boy killed in a race." That hurt so Right drew in a breath; "Known him to break out of jail to help a mare birth a big colt. He'll do."

"Mr. Taylor." Here she seemed to pull back and he knew for certain he'd spoke wrong again. "Right, you'll do also."

She put a quiet Conner Norris into his bed, plumped up the pillows and left a kerosene lamp burning on a small table. Norris had a pile of newspapers at his side, and she knew that hidden under the pillow were a pair of glasses he used to read the fine print. Old and still vain, which to her way of thinking was a healthy sign of remaining vitality. She patted his hand and he grunted; it had become their evening ritual since he'd begun to heal.

He would have been striking as a young man, with his height and those eyes, the hair she assumed had once been black and thick. She was beginning to like Con Norris and that almost angered her. It wasn't part of her training, to like her patients.

She knew exactly what she was doing when she finished cleaning in the kitchen and put on a wrap, went down to the corrals to wait. There were questions she needed answered and going to Mr. Mitchell was her only way.

He came in two hours later, the horse walking easily. Horse and rider were silhouetted against the darkened sky, lean and loose, the horse's ears nodding with each stride. She spoke first, before standing, called out his name and heard him immediately speak to the horse. Her words said over his, identifying each other.

He dismounted and immediately unsaddled the horse, who lowered his head, sighed, then let Blue scrub at his back and remove all traces of the saddle and blanket. "Ma'am, thank you for speaking up. Buck here got calmed down some but I 'spect it's still in him to spook and I ain't up for much more of that. Not tonight." He put the horse back out in the trap and the gelding stood a moment, then walked into the brush.

He moved slowly, she could see the tiredness in the way he picked up his saddle, hung the bridle on the horn. Stood a moment and she realized his hesitation before he reached down and picked up the wet and stinking saddle blanket. She studied him, noted a few scratches, a thinness to his face.

"He fought hard, didn't he, Mr. Mitchell?" "Yes, ma'am. But we worked it out. He's a good sort, just needs a reminder on occasion." She wanted to tell him that Right Taylor had said almost the exact words about him but it would be giving up a confidence.

He didn't ask but walked past her, headed to the saddle-house. She sat on the outside step and waited, hearing the ring of his spurs on the wood floor inside, the soft grunt as he lifted the gear. Then she became conscious that he stood behind her. "Ma'am." That soft voice with the indefinable accent.

"Where were you born, Mr. Mitchell?" He answered quickly, without the usual stop in his thoughts, which surprised her. "Straight west of here, maybe 200 miles." "When was the last time you were home?" "Twenty years, maybe."

Twenty years and looking at the man he would be in his mid-thirties. She had learned to read ages out here, where men Mr. Mitchell's age looked much older, and Con Norris would be ancient although she suspected he was only in his early seventies. The life here was unrelenting and deadly. But it was also a choice these men made.

She wondered, in an abstract, almost female way, if Mitchell was always so forthcoming and direct in his answers. She would guess most people never asked, since he presented a harsh and formidable front.

"Mr. Mitchell, I came to ask you why our innocent talk of colts and babies hurt you." She received a long intake of breath, a sense of him moving, then his long legs slid around her and he was outside, standing facing the night, not looking down. She waited, fascinated with a peculiar vision, of a man's bottom half, from the back, one haunch, long legs in hard wool pants, leather lining the inside of his legs, protecting his nether parts. A wise choice, she thought; the pants were wrinkled, torn in places, the leather shiny where he sat and at the inside of his knees.

He wore boots worn almost flat at the heel, and patched along the outside where a stirrup would rub. She would have to lean back and strain to see the top of him. He held that silence, and she almost spoke, to gently remind him of her question, and that it had not been meant to insult or hurt. Finally she decided to prompt him in some way, to ease her own conscience and help him perhaps find the words.

The ride had settled him physically but here it was; a few words from the nurse and his heart thumped, he couldn't think, wouldn't begin to answer. Until she stood up beside him and lightly touched a hand to his arm; "Mr. Mitchell. It is meant to be a simple question." A lie, she knew that, she was smart, educated, knew the world a whole lot better than Blue. But he knew this one thing and had never spoke the words, never let himself think on the truth.

"I have a son. Ma'am." He listened, heard that sharp gasp. "No we weren't married. She was." Deeper, a hidden pain. "I didn't know until a few years ago. He'd be seven, maybe eight years old now."

Silence, harsh breathing. "Where is he, Mr. Mitchell?" "His brother told me the boy and his ma. . .his mother they live back East. I didn't know."

She could just see his head as it turned away from her so she slowed her own breathing, tried to hear the hidden words. "Con he's sending me East with the colt. All the way to New York."

"Can you ask the brother where they are?" He went so rigid she felt he'd stopped breathing and then she remembered Right explaining about a young soldier who died and Blue was there to hold him. "No, ma'am."

Without thought her hand reached for his shoulder, her fingers felt him shudder against the touch. "Mr. Mitchell, did you love the woman?" Again he surprised her; "Yes, ma'am. More'n I thought I could." "Then the child is loved and you can give up your worries."

'Yes, ma'am' came again, even softer, and she knew he didn't believe what she said any more than she herself did. No decent man gave up worries about his child.

SIX

North Platte in Nebraska wasn't much of a town but there was a railroad line that would take the car to Chicago where it and its contents would be snapped on to a long freight going East. Through Chicago, Blue was told, then around some lakes and into New York. The trip might take a week, with the transfers and the rest stops. The new owner of Brush Fire, known as Curly, made all the arrangement; it was for Blue to get to North Platte leading the colt and by god nothing bad better happen between here and there. The insurance went into effect when the colt was loaded and signed onto the private rail car.

Blue listened to Con's bluster and knew exactly what he'd do, who he would pick to ride with him. All the time Con was talking, spewing out curses and excitement, Blue stood quiet, not wanting to take in the words.

The woman's question last night had brought out all his fears, and listening to Con didn't help much. Blue had no defense against what had been stirred up except to think of a good horse and the far mountains and let the man's fretting blow right over him.

He figured he'd go easy with the colt, stops for grazing, good water, no hurry. Blue didn't know quite why but he trusted Haney, who would keep his mouth shut and watch careful, and Rhynes was showing a curiosity and wanting to know about horses and not how to ride them to a sweaty standstill but how to keep them calm and get more out of them.

Blue asked for the two men as guards, Con shrugged, said it was Blue's choice. Both men agreed, Haney with his usual grunt and Rhynes with a peculiar light in his eyes that had Blue puzzled until he got caught up in packing gear and figuring out how to get where he was going.

The morning Blue was to set out, the crew was missing one man. Blake, gear packed, private horse caught and saddled; the man was long gone from the tracks. No note, nothing. The abrupt disappearance made Blue restless; he'd never gotten a sense of Blake other than the man was a fool around horses. His leaving meant only one man could ride with Blue. Haney had to stay behind; Rhynes became the choice as guard. Right made that decision and it wasn't to Blue's comfort but then he had more faith in Right than he had suspicion of Rhynes.

It occured to Blue that Rhynes might be thinking about $10,000 walking in front of him, jigging some of the time, lifting his tail to drop a thin line of manure, snorting and trying to bite Blue's steady dun gelding. The dun told the much younger colt with a quick snap of his own teeth against the colt's hide that such behavior was not to be tolerated.

It felt good to Blue to be on the dun. He rode the horse for easy ranch work and the good dun was steady and reliable, slowed down from his racing days but still a formidable opponent for the chestnut colt. Blue's nightmare was the colt getting loose; hell no one'd ever catch the youngster out here in these miles of sandy hills and high grass excepting maybe the dun in his younger days.

The trail went through soft hills, around prairie dog holes, dry creek beds and even a railroad crossing where it took extra time to get the colt over his suspicion of the shiny rails, strange smells and the crunch of cinders underfoot. The colt wanted to jump, but would never clear all the tracks so Blue snubbed his head tight to the dun and got bitten for his efforts but they walked across careful and safe after a few doubtful minutes.

Rhynes came along behind, on a steady gray Con often used on roundup. Rhynes had nothing to say, showed no impatience when Blue let the colt sniff and paw and finally give in.

A bored man stood at the doorway to a small mercantile, as if the collection of three buildings and a wandering thread of water made for a town. When Blue got the colt over the tracks, the man saluted, spoke his few words. "Good looker that one, handful ain't he." Blue laughed and let the dun out into an easy lope, hauling the chestnut colt along.

Well away from the buildings, Blue brought the dun back to a walk, rubbed some at his leg where the colt had bitten into muscle. Rhynes came up on the off side, away from the colt. He nodded once to Blue but kept his own thoughts. The quiet suited Blue just fine.

They had no schedule for the 130-mile trip, slow miles, time to graze, night camp for the men and rest for the horses. Blue settled in a good trot, let the colt bounce and tugged some, knowing the youngster was seeing the grasslands as his playground, where he could run out all his energy.

A half-hour later the trot had smoothed and there was no word yet from Rhynes, who stayed off to the side and back, rifle held lightly across the saddle. It was a relief to not have to tell the man his work; Rhynes knew to take point on his own. Blue figured the man had cavalry in his past, but he didn't bother to ask. Sometimes all it took was one word and a man opened up and blathered until the listener wanted to cover his ears and shout. Rhynes didn't look the type, but Blue wasn't taking chances.

Supper was beans and coffee, the horses hobbled close by, the colt tired enough to sleep standing, then wake to nibble at grass. Can't push him too hard, Blue thought, he's still a youngster.

"He is that, Mitchell. But he moves right well." The voice startled Blue and he half rose, grabbed his close-by rifle until he realized it was only Rhynes talking. He settled back and felt like a goddamn fool; Rhynes nodded, "Just agreeing with you. That's a good 'un but he's still young. Not like these range-bred broncs, hell you ride 'em at two, they quit at ten and you catch up another. That there son'll make his mark, beat everything he comes against and be servicing them mares to make more like him. Not a bad life, if you can run like that son there."

He'd been right in his guess; open up Rhynes and all kinds of words came out.

The man seemed to be studying the colt too long and that made Blue nervous. He told Rhynes to take first watch; Blue'd sleep, then spell him. It was a fool's thought for Blue stayed awake, hand on the pistol under his blanket, eyes watching the shape of Rhynes not too far from camp.

But when Rhynes came to wake him, Blue was sleeping, convinced he'd watched half the night. Rhynes called his name, then stepped back, waited, and Blue sat up confused, blanket pulled off, hand still gripped on the pistol.

"I thought you might think that way, Mitchell. Don't shoot me, I ain't worth it. I couldn't handle that colt, nevermind run with him knowing you'd be chasing me. Hell, Mitchell, I'd have to kill you and it ain't in my nature."

Blue cleared his head, remembered thinking earlier that Rhynes might be quiet most of the time but when he got started, he would have a rough go coming to the end.

Blue nodded, laid the pistol across his hand and offered it to Rhynes. "You sleep with her now; I'll take the watch and the rifle." It was his way of making apology. And Rhynes laughed as he accepted the peculiar gift. They were square now. But only until morning.

Blue went a fair distance upwind of the horses and camp, checking on the chestnut colt and the dun, paying no attention to the stocky gray that Rhynes had saddled. That horse would take care of himself and any thief set on taking him would have a fight. Con liked spirit in the horses he bred, said it came from the first horse he stood to stud. A mustang, a dark bay with heart who stamped all his get, down through generations, with toughness and spirit and damned good legs. Blue agreed with the man and it was another reason he'd stayed on to work for him.

Tonight was stars and black sky, a soft wind, smell of water in the air, lonesome and filled with small noises, rustles and squeals, midnight talk that let a man know he wasn't pure alone.

It rained unexpectedly two days later, sheets coming straight from the south, headed north over Blue and Rhynes and the chestnut colt. The colt objected, shook his head, ears twisted, mane soaked. He refused to step forward against the wind, wanting to swing his butt and stand head down, waiting through the storm. The two ridden horses were in agreement, but spurs and a hand on the bridle reins kept them steadied.

It was a hard-fought few miles through the blow, shortening Blue's temper, but the storm's fury had the advantage of silencing Rhynes completely. The rain kept coming until camp was made in a small ravine, up against the banking. The horses stood quiet, tails to the wind, heads down, all three pushed close for warmth and safety, forgetting their differences until the storm broke.

Blue eyed Rhynes as if considering the same situation and the man grinned, said, "Don't think so." Blue answered, "Me neither, you just ain't that pretty." They managed to keep a small fire going, feeding it dried grasses and bent brush pulled out of the banking. They got it hot enough to boil coffee and pretended they were almost warm. They both slept some, but jerked awake at the few sounds heard over the wind.

Morning was bright sun and shivering horses. Rhynes patrolled the banking to find bushes out of their reach last night, while Blue attempted to cook up bacon and boil stale coffee., Nothing needed to be said; coffee and bacon, and the horses standing in sunshine, grazing now, the colt lying down for a half hour's sleep.

Then it was time to move out; both men scraped wet off drying hide and saddled up. Blue held to the colt's line, and glanced at Rhynes. If he looked as bad as his riding escort, both men would scare any decent folk. He sighed, nodded and gigged the dun into a slow trot. They had time to make up, but there'd been no choice.

The land was treeless, rolling with high grasses that the horses snatched at, chewed on as they moved out. Blue'd rode Charley with only a bosal today, and saw that Rhynes had made the same decision. Had to be a decent man if he thought that much on his horse's comfort.

They rode at a walk, letting the horses graze the high grasses, careful round any thick mud places, letting the deep sun warm them, dry their clothes and ease their minds.

It was a rare moment of quiet, soaking in the morning, knowing secretly that by noon they would be hot and cranky but the sweet air and easy gait almost put both men to sleep. The horses moved slowly, gracefully, chewing without greed or urgency.

Tall spires of mounded sand rose on either side of the faint trail, and the horses followed the slow downward slant of grass, finally joining a wider trail covered with small split tracks. Pronghorn, Blue decided, and took an extra hold on the colt's lead. If a small herd jumped up in front of them, the Thoroughbred colt would by his nature spook and try to bolt.

He was busy coiling in the rope, setting his hand to the loops, when a voice stunned him and the horses stopped, the colt half-reared and Blue almost came out of the dun's saddle. "Rhynes, you get over here. Mitchell, you're done. Give me that horse." He knew the voice; Blake. Horse stealing planned in advance.

He got himself together, reached for his pistol, searching for Rhynes and knowing the bitter fact of betrayal. Should of known, he'd felt something was wrong. Blue swung Charley around, intent on finding Blake, then Rhynes, and shooting both of them.

His eyes focused, saw Blake's ugly face, the features tighten, a pistol come up barrel straight at Blue. He shuddered, Charley half-reared and Blake fired. The bullet hit Charley in the neck and dropped him, hauling Blue under the carcass, hand pulled high to keep hold of the colt. He was yanked, twisted, his leg caught under Charley's ribs, his arm overhead, shoulder aching as the colt fought back, pawed and reared in terror.

Then another shot too close and Blue expected a blow, a new pain, the colt to drop on top of him but it was followed by a second shot and a grunt, then a howl and he could hear a running horse until that sound, too, disappeared. His arm was lowered, the colt stopped pulling and it was quiet. Too quiet; Charley had stopped breathing, the barest movement was blood pooling under the dun's neck, soaking Blue's arm and side.

He closed his eyes, shuddered again. Then a voice startled him; "Mitchell, you alive ain't you?" Rhynes, he thought, it didn't sound like Blake but the tone was familiar. It had to be Rhynes, but Blake had called to the man for help.

He opened his eyes, Rhynes all right. Blue coughed, spat blood, not his, at least he didn't think so. "Get me out of this." Rhynes nodded, dropped a rope over the saddle horn, Blue held to the colt and used his left hand to secure the rope. "Pull the dun off me damn it and don't stop if I yell, hell man it hurts."

Rhynes nodded and set up the gray, let the horse steady himself, then backed him quickly, lifting Charley's corpse enough so that Blue crawled out, still holding to the colt who was bugged-eye but motionless.

Blue stood, bent sideways, walked to the colt who snorted and shivered and listened to Blue's words. Finally he lowered his head and stuck out his nose and Blue could touch him.

Even that hurt; he recognized cracked ribs, a bruised eye and his arm, hell it must be two inches longer from holding to the colt. He turned, keeping a hand on the colt's shoulder. Rhynes sat that blocky gray, rope snug to Blue's good saddle, Charley's flesh pulled and laid out like nothing ever alive.

"Thanks, Rhynes. What the hell happened?" The man touched the gray's sides and the horse let up the tension, the dun corpse flopped back and the colt started to jump but Blue's hand kept him quiet.

"Guess ole Blake thought he could take your colt, heard that price the boss was getting and figured it was his. I didn't know the man that well, had no idea he'd turn bad."

Blue rubbed his face. "Can you hold on to the colt and let that gray pull up. . .Charley again. I need my gear." It was done in silence; Blue yanked the bridle from the dun's skull, stepped in blood to loosen the off latigo, drag the saddle and blanket, and his few belongings from the dead animal.

Blue was breathing in short hard gasps when he was done, and Rhynes eased the dead horse to lie back against the matted grass. He untied the colt and handed the lines to Blue. "Guess we need to bury Blake. I killed him." Nothing sounded in the voice as Rhynes discussed the practical matter. Blue waited, tried to breathe without hurting, shivered some, then looked up at Rhynes.

For the first time Rhynes was able to meet Blue's stare as Blue spoke his mind; "Me, I don't think much of a man set to kill another over a horse ain't his own. I got cracked ribs. You want that man buried, you best tend to it. It's going to be all I can do to saddle and ride this colt and I'm betting he's gonna to get out of here fast."

There was a hesitation in Rhynes, the flickering eyes shifted to one side, then back to staring at Blue. The voice was low and thick but the words were clear. "I killed him, I'll bury him. Even the enemy deserves that much." The sentiment surprised Blue.

He sat some distance from the digging and burying, watching as Rhynes worked with a quickly dulled knife and the few rocks he could find in the sandy ground. The two horses stood together, the colt hobbled, the gray willing to stand ground-tied, hipshot, eyes closed. Occasionally the youngster would nip at his companion and the gray would squeal, bite hard on the colt's hide and then they settled again. It took Rhynes an hour to finish his chore.

There was no sign of Blake's horse; just a limp body, a ruined face, too much blood and loose matter. Blue turned away; he'd been here before.

SEVEN

He'd been right; Rhynes had to saddle the colt for him; Blue couldn't lift his own rig without getting stuck. Damn.

When he mounted and the colt reared, Blue went limp above the neck and withers and his weight brought the unbalanced youngster down to standing only briefly before bolting. Blue let him run; he didn't blame the colt and couldn't stop him if he tried. He rode hunch over to protect himself.

Rhynes came along behind the pair at an easy lope, knowing better than to challenge the Thoroughbred. When the colt finally slowed as Blue circled him, Rhynes had the gray at a walk and the chestnut slid in beside his new best buddy, pleased enough to be with the gray, with anyone, that he rested his muzzle on the gray's neck and did not try to bite.

One look at Blue and Rhynes knew to keep quiet. There was smeared blood at his mouth, the side of his face that hit the ground was bruised and swelling. But the man rode easier now, almost smiling.

"Don't think nothing's open, just sore. We'll make up time tomorrow." Rhynes was uncomfortable with the entire matter. Mitchell didn't make it any easier on him.

"You saved my life. Thanks." Rhynes nodded as he turned his head away. He'd help kill that boy, now he'd shot a man to save another life. It was rough finding the reason for two deaths by his hand. Yeah he'd been in the Army, taught to kill, rode out to kill, but it was battle, usually for a cause. This was death to a man he'd known, ridden with, yet he could not let Blake kill Mitchell.

The whole matter confused him, so he hid in silence, knowing that Mitchell preferred quiet while he worked a horse.

And he was working that colt, hands spread wide, a rein in each one, a bit in the colt's mouth, no easy bosal this time. Asking that mouth to give, the neck to bend, putting the colt sideways, then to the other direction. Once Mitchell looked up and grinned and Rhynes shook his head. Mitchell's voice was dry and thin but he had his say.

"If I leave him be after that runaway, he'll think it's the way life is. I earn my keep teaching him to listen and obey. He's a big boy now. Time to grow up, he's got to know how to behave in company."

Rhynes ducked his head, Blue rode the colt in a small circle and above them birds flew their own path; the sky was quiet and the riders were alone.

There was no need for words until dusk, when Blue motioned to a wash and a good cutbank. "If it storms again. . ." Both men glanced at the darkening sky heavy with rain. Rhynes nodded. They unsaddled, and the colt groaned. Blue felt badly for him, he was a youngster, just three years and a few months and this long riding carrying a stock saddle and Blue's weight wasn't good for him.

There was no choice. Blue's ribs and the side of his face reminded him of how close he'd come. He couldn't help but glance at Rhynes, working through the same chore, taking time to wad up grass and scour the gray's back, clean it of sweat and dust. He'd wondered all the long, slowed afternoon about Rhynes and Blake and maybe their working together. Now he knew.

Supper was burned beans and weak coffee and neither man seemed to care. One airtight of peaches shared between them eased the tension. But each move Blue made was a reminder, and the halter and lead tied to the saddle was proof. One horse dead, one rider meant to die. A thief buried in high grass.

There were stars now, and a light breeze carrying a sweet scent but no rain. Rhynes opened the silence; "I was part of it." The words stuttered, halted, then he coughed, continued; "I didn't know it would come to that, to him dying. It wasn't what we planned." He gulped and looked away from the firelight. "There ain't no excuse. I couldn't bear riding with you and not speaking up. It was my fault and I've paid for it."

No names, no details but Blue had guessed, watching Rhynes all the afternoon, in a daze part of the time from the ribs, the bruising, the fury at a good horse's death. More death; it was then he connected the face with a past time, other dyings. Death was coupled with Rhynes' endless talking when he did speak. Blue raged inside as he tried to think clearly; if Rhynes had been working with Blake, he would have let the man shoot Blue instead of killing the man, and now making his confession.

Rhynes sat upright, away from the solid banking, hands laid wide apart, palms up, a gesture of peace, a show of reluctance to fight. It was for Blue to decide. His voice was rough, thoughts pushing at him.

"I figured something. You looked too familiar. . .I thought this afternoon. I wasn't sure." The two men deliberately did not look at each other. It was a place Blue'd never been, wanting to forgive a man for killing something he'd come to love. The word itself spooked him; too much surrounded the boy and his death; his mother, her child, the boy's half brother. Blue's son. Too much.

Rhynes' head dropped, his hands moved, then retreated. "I ain't killed since, until today. It was you I was saving, I couldn't let you get killed, not till I told you. We didn't mean the boy to die that way."

Blue asked; "Did Sutter know. . .?" Rhynes shook his head. "It was Davenport, he got us involved, talked me into holding back water. It was wrong, I knew it then, I can't. . ." In heavy silence they sought their own edge of the embankment, Blue getting up twice through the night to check on the horses.

They'd covered more ground that expected, the colt running away shortened the needed days, then again they'd lost hours from the rain. Tomorrow they would ride into North Platte. He had to sort out what he'd just learned before he and Rhynes parted.

The morning was heavy; thick air, some fog, and it was hard starting the fire for coffee. Rhynes gave up in disgust; Blue knelt and slowly fed a small spark, got the wood going. Soon enough the boiling coffee brought a few words from each man.

Rhynes stared straight at Blue this time; "I ain't asking forgiveness of you, Mr. Mitchell, no one can forgive such a death. I only want you to know. His face haunts me at night."

Blue hesitated, the chestnut colt whinnied at the words, the gray moved restlessly. It was past time to saddle up. He kept his back to Rhynes; "Me, I thought on this last night, I set up some." Rhynes nodded. Blue gave himself a moment, unsure of what he wanted to say, how to say it. He'd fought himself to accept the boy's death, now to meet up with the man who'd been part of the killing; hell he wasn't a good enough man to handle it.

He'd sought his own forgiveness and hadn't come to it yet. Talking up the bay's speed, comparing the two half-brother duns, ganging up on Sutter. This was how Blue had brought the boy to his death. It would take a lifetime to find his own forgiveness, yet he could help this one man suffering similar doubts and anger.

So he said all that he could, to one of Josh's killers; "It was a mistake you made, a bad choice. I've made some bad choices myself. It was a horse race and Josh told me he knew the risks and could accept them."

It was all he could manage. Rhynes poured out coffee, Blue took a cup, sipped at it. Bitter, filled with grounds. About what they both deserved.

"How're the ribs?" This was Rhynes' poor attempt at talk, getting them away from what haunted them. "Sore." The one word was all Blue could handle. Filled with pain, regret, and full anger at himself.

Mitchell chose a long trot after ten minutes of walking. Rhynes kept the gray to the cowboy's left, watching the swollen face for clues. The colt seemed willing in the beginning, asking with tugs on the reins for a gallop, a bit of freedom, but Mitchell kept the colt to his job, and Rhynes ended up setting the gray's lope as the stocky horse didn't have the trot that colt could produce.

In time, Mitchell slowed the colt and let both horses walk. There was sweat on the man's face, under his arms, down his back, and yet the air was cool and Rhynes himself was hardly bothered by the ride. The gray too was damp but not lathered.

By his reckoning, Mitchell had to be suffering through those cracked ribs.

No words, nothing, only hard breathing and a hand once to his side, pressing something deep. Rhynes cleared his throat and Mitchell didn't swing around to look at him so he kept that particular thought to himself.

They hit a sandy stretch down a hillside marked with small holes. Not prairie dogs, not that kind of mound, but tiny burrows with feathers, a few bones pushed away from each opening. Rhynes wondered out loud; surprisingly Mitchell answered.

"They're owls. I know it looks strange but they burrow and choose this as their town. Guess they're like us, they make a choice and have to live with it."

Then Mitchell turned and studied Rhynes. "I don't mean to be lecturing, just talking facts about them owls." It was all right, the words weren't intended to be a goad under Rhynes' touchy hide.

Eventually they rode into a flat marsh that covered one side of a shimmering pool. It was almost a lake, with narrow trails leading to the edges like spokes off a wheel. Birds everywhere, long-legged white birds that flew up in elegant panic as the two horses sidestepped the marsh and reach into the lake to lower their heads and drink. The colt didn't bother to shy or spook as the birds rose in flight, he was thirsty and tired and all that mattered was water.

Finally they reined the horses out of the lake and then Mitchell asked a favor, something Rhynes knew was downright misery for the man. The horses stood close, relaxed, dozing and content. Without looking at him, Mitchell spoke; "Rhynes, we need filled canteens." Rhynes heard the tired voice crack; "I can't climb down and then get back on." He gave Rhynes his canteen and it was easy to see the shaking hand, the fresh beads of sweat on the man's forehead and jaw.

Rhynes slipped off the gray and handed one rein to Mitchell before doing the simple chore. Bad enough riding horseback, but Mitchell faced a long train ride and it sure as hell wasn't going to be a pleasure.

The sun beat at an angle into their eyes as the beginnings of North Platte showed; high chimneys, distant noise, small roads that came together forming a larger, wider path. To the edge was a narrow trail carrying hoof prints and lines of dried manure.

Blue gestured for Rhynes to go ahead, letting the tired colt walk slowly behind the gray. A few minutes later Rhynes heard odd noises and glanced behind him to find Mitchell walking, leading the colt whose head was low, ears loose. The man grunted at times, but he only shook his head and gestured to go on when Rhynes tried to rein in his own horse. Offered up the gray, willing to do the walking for Mitchell. He got a stronger grunt, a slight headshake, and a quick grin. That would do for both no and thanks.

They came in on the west side of town, near the railroad yard. The colt threw his head up at the first steam whistle but had no energy left to fight or run. A tug on the reins, a few words from Mitchell and the colt kept walking.

Guess the hard ride had done the colt some good.

Con had given him directions coming in from the north to the rail yard. Mr. Belmont himself had a private car built to carry his best racehorses, and he'd sent that car to pick up Curly for his trip East. Con figured it would be easy enough to find the car; the durned thing would stand out from the labeled freight and passenger cars painted with names of the local railroad lines.

With the chestnut colt this tired, Blue decided he'd stall him the night in the car, get the colt used to his new surroundings while he was still wore out. He hoped the train stopped a few times on this trip; traveling with a hot-blooded three year old wasn't Blue's idea of an easy journey.

He had his own fears; he too had never been on a train, never been East, hell Denver and Trinidad and even Tucson were the biggest cities he'd been in. He'd heard stories, thought most of them were tall tales but deep inside he knew those men were speaking a truth they'd witnessed and it awed them.

Then there had been those newspapers with their illustrations and Blue decided he had to take what looked like a tall tale as the truth; buildings he couldn't imagine, streets and street cars and even automobiles, all things he didn't want in his life but they were here, now, and he'd have to deal with them. All these thoughts scared him half to death. At least the sore ribs, the slowly-healing face gave Blue something other than the train ride to occupy his thoughts.

A train engine rumbled across a set of tracks and the colt reared, settled and then leaned against Rhynes' equally tired gray. Blue held to the lead, almost as spooked as the colt. He looked up into Rhynes' widened eyes and the two men laughed. Hell they'd both seen a train engine before, just never got this close to the power and sound.

A sign half-hanging by a loosened nail said it was the railway office, so Blue guessed he'd go inside and let the man know Mr. Belmont's fine race horse had arrived.

Jeptha didn't look up; it was coming nighttime and his relief wasn't here and now some cowboy come in wanting something, hat in hand, looking beat up and oh lord Jeptha didn't want to bother with helping no one. He wanted to go home to supper and a set in their one stuffed chair, watching his wife with the children, maybe chewing on one of those cigars a man brung him all the way from Chicago.

Being yard master gave him a few small pleasures; whiskey once from a fine man's private car, a bottle of something sparkling from France, said so right there on the thick glass, and these cigars. Now these he could take a real liking to. He didn't drink much so the whiskey and that bubbly stuff hadn't been too great a pleasure except in being given them; the cigars, well, he sure could make them a habit, even over his wife's direction that he smoke them outside. Right now, he said, well no, it'd been raining these past weeks, then it was too damned chilly at night, getting warmer so he might put a rocking chair outside and take his smoke in the cool evening. The doing so would make her happier, and he'd get more pleasure from the smoke without her words chewing at him.

"Mister." There was a tightness to the single word. Jeptha resisted looking up, he had a schedule to finish, and was half-listening for the sounds of Bobby's boots outside, telling him his relief was here and it was time to go home.

A hand placed itself across the papers, so close to Jeptha's eyes that he could see every crease and bruise, old scarring and breaks, without putting on the glasses he normally used to read. "Mister. I need directions to August Belmont's horse car. It's waiting on me and what I got to deliver."

Oh. Well. That's where these fine cigars came from. Oh dear, well, he guessed it was all right and finally looked up. Yes indeed the face was battered, one side quite swollen, but the sheer malice and determination that shined out of those eyes was enough to make Jeptha push back in his chair that thankfully had wheels, and put some distance between himself and this rather threatening stranger.

Yet it occurred to him later that it took a man such as this Blue Mitchell, as he finally introduced himself, what a peculiar name, it took this hardheaded type of westerner to escort a valuable horse across a wild country full of unspeakable dangers. It would be a very angry Mr. August Belmont if the horse were taken illegally, and most likely such a theft would mean the life of Mr. Mitchell in any battle between him and horse thieves.

Upon studying Mr. Mitchell, and then looking out through the opened door to the waiting horses, Jeptha decided he would pity any horse thief who had designs on the character and abilities of a rather lean and scared-looking chestnut colt who stood close to a sturdy gray horse. Gelding, he reminded himself, not an entire horse. He had been told the difference; that a horse meant a stallion, a mare was female, a gelding had no testicles and therefore no amorous ambitions. Jeptha knew what his wife would say if he dared explain these differences.

He stood slowly, well behind the desk in case his reading of Mr. Mitchell's temper was incorrect. The man seemed to understand Jeptha's nervousness, for he held his hands open, backed up and grinned; "I don't mean you no harm, mister, I just want to get the colt onto that boxcar."

Out here, away from city influence and common manners, Jeptha had learned to take note of certain men who carried a strength accepting no interference. He quickly decided that Blue Mitchell was one of those men, and sighed with relief, even more eager to go home to the safety of his family.

Having shown Mitchell and the chestnut colt, and another man on a quiet horse, to the aforementioned boxcar, Jeptha decided it would be proper if he stayed to watch, to make certain the colt was safely bedded. He found himself holding his breath as Mitchell led the hot-tempered, obviously well-bred chestnut up close to the ramp into the fitted boxcar.

The horse initially resisted stepping on the wooden ramp, a decidedly intelligent act, Jeptha thought. He expected some yelling, a rope or two, a lot of pushing and swearing to get that colt up into the car.

When, unexpectedly, Mitchell stopped and sat down on the edge of the ramp, Jeptha decided to stay a few moments longer and watch. This was highly unusual behavior.

Rhynes knew to set on the gray and wait. He felt his own bones ache, his gut rumble; he was durn near eaten through with hunger and the remains of attempted horse-theft, but he wanted to watch Mitchell move that colt onto the ramp and up its steep angle into the dark interior of the car. He bet to himself it would take the man less than fifteen minutes.

He almost gave up before he started counting since Blue led the colt to the ramp and sat down, didn't look at the colt or tug at the line but sat quiet, rubbed his jaw, touched gently around the swollen eye and pulled off his hat to expose fading blond hair, shook it free and then the colt took a step, sort of nipped at the hair and Blue grinned, raised one hand up to the colt's muzzle. The colt seemed to put pressure on Blue's hand, and the two of them rested on each other.

Another minute or two, the colt put his head down and sniffed the wooden ramp, with its cross bars that would give his hooves purchase on the otherwise slick wood. Blue still made no move, other than to touch the colt's neck. Then he stood, turned, clucked to the colt and started up the ramp.

The colt hesitated, then put a hoof on the wooden ramp, snorted, Blue stopped, didn't look back but spoke something in a low voice and the colt leaped halfway up the ramp, standing ahead of Blue, who walked on past the colt into the dark interior of the car and the colt followed as if he'd been doing this his whole life.

Rhynes nodded to himself and then grinned at Jeptha; "Wish you'd been a betting man, mister. I give him fifteen minutes in my head and I'd guess now it was less than ten."

Jeptha shivered, drew his coat closer although the evening was mild to quite warm, and went home, to think over what he had seen a rough cowboy straight off the Nebraska plains do with a young and obviously fancy-bred racing horse. It was more than he could fathom.

One end of the car was boarded off; slats a good two inches thick ran against the walls, held mid-way against a stout post running to the roof. There were inches showing between each slat which Blue didn't trust. He'd seen horses get a hoof caught in a smaller space, yanked hell out of a leg, tore tendons and broke bones. It would do for the night, but tomorrow while they waited on the train schedule, he'd rearrange the boards more to his liking. They had everything nailed to the outside of the supports – damn fools, any decent horse could push against that and those nails would slide out and damn they'd have a horse loose inside a boxcar with no way to control him.

Whoever designed and built this traveling circus knew a lot more about making things pretty than actually keeping a horse inside a pen. The wood was polished and the nails sunk in and smoothed over but the whole thing wouldn't hold the colt for long.

The pen was bedded nice, though, with lots of straw, a rick filled with good hay. He led the colt inside, over to the hay, picked up a fistful and sniffed it; sweet and fresh. He shook the handful and only few seeds fell out, no burned or moldy leaves. It would do for the journey. He'd already decided it was best not to grain the colt but keep hay in front of him all the time, water too, and he'd clean out the dirty straw, replace it from the pile in a corner where he figured he'd bed down too.

With the slats dropped in to close the doorway, Blue felt comfortable enough to find Rhynes and his good gray where they still waited. He walked down the ramp, conscious of a banging and a whinny from inside the car. Rhynes looked at him expectantly; they had no more orders, only told to get the colt to the railhead on time.

Blue rubbed his swollen face; "Bring that gray inside, let him stay next to the colt, help settle him. You up to finding us some grub before you bed for the night?" Rhynes nodded, Blue handed him two of the silver dollars Con had given him. "Buy some cans for me, it's best I don't leave the colt at any stop for feeding, so I'll take whatever you can find. Thanks."

They eyed each other; it had been a tough journey, with revelations and occurrences neither of them anticipated. Now the unexpected closeness of two men battling the same damaged conscience would dissolve over the next month or so.

Still, for a few moments talk, Blue felt more settled in his own guilt, and hoped for Rhynes' soul that he'd found the same relief.

EIGHT

The first lurch sent Blue's coffee spilling onto his legs and the colt squealed, kicked out and took a chunk of splinters from the makeshift stall. The colt charged forward on the second lurch, and the third had him sitting on his haunches, eyes wild and rimmed in white, neck and hindquarters darkening with sweat.

Blue managed to stand between the push and pull, throwing what was left of the coffee into a pile of rustling, shifting straw. Damn.

He lifted two of the slats that made the stall barrier and stood inside the pen, leaning against the wall to keep his balance. His voice was low, jerked at times by the train's acceleration but he talked to the colt, told him he was scared too, that it was his first ride on a train, never been here before, didn't know what the hell was going on and wished he had open prairie and grass underfoot instead of this slippery wood and not enough straw but they was stuck here for a few days.

As he watched the colt struggle to keep his footing, Blue decided next time this nightmare came to a halt longer'n twenty minutes, he'd pull the colt's shoes, give him a trim, had to be tools somewhere inside these rail yards where folks still used horses to move things from place to place. It hadn't come to him that the colt would slip on the wood flooring; he'd never had a horse stalled before excepting through that winter when he broke colts for a man someplace in Colorado.

That had been a dirt floor, stinking with piss and manure and it was his job to clean out what he could and ride whatever was given to him in exchange for staying warm that winter and eating two meals a day.

Now he was angry at himself, watching the colt slide, legs spread too wide, eyes holding a terrible panic. Even worse it came to Blue that if the colt could get his legs under him, then he might take a leap at the stall barrier.

He risked stepping away from the solid wood to touch the colt's neck and rub the shoulder, and that bright chestnut head came around, the muzzle opened and teeth bit Blue's arm but he only laughed and stroked the damp neck and the colt then kind of leaned on Blue and slowly the wide dark eyes eased until no more white showed.

"All right there, Curly, we're in this together."

The gray's presence had eased the colt's fears through the night and gave Blue time to find wood and a hammer, nails, that he borrowed from an old man setting to a chair, smoking a pipe, nodding as Blue asked permission, said he'd be sure that Jeptha Wilson put the cost of that there wood on Mr. Belmont's Jr.'s bill, and 'yes sir, I trust you to return the tools.' Blue nodded to the old man, and struggled back to the railcar with his find.

He had to go back out to the old man to ask for a saw; the wide face grinned around the clenched pipe; "Was wondering how you figured to cut them boards all the same length without no saw." The man's easy humor made it simple for Blue to not get angry over the second trip and the old man's amusement on his account. He wasn't use to borrowing.

He'd spent all that time in the morning rebuilding the poorly designed stall; he sure didn't like stalls but the colt had to be kept confined. Blue did all the building with Curly trying to help, taking the hammer when Blue laid it down, nuzzling at the borrowed saw which bit back and the colt curled his lip, pushed at the saw then spooked to the far corner when the metal fell and rang a short tune. Too bad he hadn't thought about shoes and wood floors and wet urine when there was extra time.

Now as he watched the colt bang around the confining stall, he was glad he'd made the effort. Those pretty planed and smoothed and stained boards on the front would never have kept the colt inside.

He grinned, seeing the old man's face, smelling the harsh bitter smoke. Now there was a habit he hadn't brought with him;

needing to smoke in a rail car filled with straw and hay would surely be a problem.

When the train settled into its rhythm and each wheel hit the steel meeting of the track lines, rocking the car gently and quickly, he found himself swaying, then unsettled, so he climbed out of the colt's stall and sat down, back to the boarded stall opening, leaving the top rail pulled back. Each jerk of the car couplings hit an ache in his chest; damn it those ribs were still mending from the fall and a train ride wasn't going to help them heal. Then he had to laugh; he'd been hurt worse and he'd got over it. No different this time, or any of those times still to happen. He'd bet on it, if he were a betting man.

The colt found this small open place and he arched his neck over the remaining boards and rested his muzzle on Blue's head.

"No Curly, you don't chew up there. That ain't the hay or straw and there ain't much left so leave it be." The colt must have pulled back his lips for Blue felt the rigid teeth press into his skull and he raised a hand, felt the pressure lessen and then he laughed. There wasn't much he could do about his hair thinning, and blaming the colt for pretending to graze was a waste of time.

"All right, Curly, you want to try, well go ahead." He lowered his hand, the colt snuffled, snorted, Blue felt a tug and then the weight of the colt's muzzle, lips compressed, rested companionably on his skull.

They rode for hours it seemed, until Blue knew he had to stand up or he'd be found frozen stiff in one place, unable to move at all. Whoever put the car together for hauling horses these distances knew a few things other than how to confine them. Two big wood barrels stood braced in a corner; he could hear the water move, could smell it when a few drops got spilled through the tight lid. And there was enough hay for a herd of range horses, guess they figured the colt would be half-starved by his upbringing.

William A. Luckey

It was a struggle but he stood, stretched some, careful of his ribs, then took the colt's empty bucket and tried walking to the barrels. It was another dance of forward and sideways and he thought he might get a bellyache from the swaying but soon enough he learned to let his knees bend and go soft in his back, kind of like riding a bronc, giving to the lurches instead of tightening against them.

Watered, drinking only when Blue held the bucket, the colt turned to his hay, swaying with the car and no longer in terror. Blue found a particularly soft pile of straw and took himself a nap.

They stopped once somewhere Blue didn't recognize. A man pulled open the heavy middle door, calling out as he yanked up the iron latch. The colt answered with a loud whinny that had Blue laughing when the door slid open and the inside was flooded with light. He blink, yawned, saw that the colt was doing the same. Man called out; "How you doing in there?"

First voice he'd heard in hours, interrupting his nap and he wasn't use to naps but he preferred them to people. So he approached the opened door, appreciated the steadiness of the standing car floor, shied from the light and asked; "Where are we? Is there time to get the colt off for a walk?" The man looked up at him, scratched his head. "Hell we're just east of North Platte, mister. You got yourself a long ride ahead and no there ain't time to take that race horse off the car, we're stopped for a herd of cattle crossing, be ready to move out in a moment."

The door was dragged shut, the heavy latch sounding like a cell door slammed with him inside. Blue remembered a few days of being locked in a cell, on two or three occasions when he'd lost his temper or stepped outside some petty law in his younger days. Especially he remembered the sound of the guard house door at Fort Robinson, all because he'd caught a Thoroughbred stallion carrying an officer's brand. When he thought on the facts, it seemed he hadn't spent his years in the best of company.

70

He turned to the colt; "Guess we got us some long hours ahead." The colt nodded as if agreeing, then yawned and Blue settled himself in to ride out the bothersome grinding jerks as the train yanked and pulled at itself until all the cars slid on those shiny tracks, headed someplace Blue'd never been and didn't want to go. He was doing this for Con.

It went like that, stop and start, lurch and clack and Blue had no time sense of day or night. He tried peering through the boxcar slats, sometimes it looked like day and then the train went on and it was too suddenly dark. He figured out the change in light and sudden dark meant they'd gone through a city or town along the line and suddenly were back in the open country.

They did stop once for two hours, outside of Chicago the brakeman said, and Blue pulled the colt's shoes but didn't dare take him off the train. He'd had nightmares of the colt escaping and there'd be no way to get him back.

Thankfully Mr. Belmont had a man waiting in Chicago, and a few days of planned stop so the colt could get out and run. The man was a Negro, small, long arms and big hands and a quiet face. He almost looked familiar to Blue but he couldn't place him. Blue had no particular feelings about Negroes; he'd ridden alongside them in other races and on different ranches, sat and ate with a few over lonesome campfires but he'd never met one individual. Then again he didn't make friends often.

This man took no notice of Blue but spoke his piece, saying he would take over the colt and get him to the stables for a few days and Blue shook his head, said he'd been given the colt to get to New York safely and by God unless August Belmont Junior himself came up and told him different, then he was with the colt the whole journey.

The man studied him, having to step back and look up to see into Blue's face. Usually that started an argument, but this man seemed to have a different idea about Blue and his word.

His voice was soft with no apology in the words or his manner; "Well now sir, I reckon you best come 'long with me.

71

You sure you ain't wanting to see some of this good city while I take care of the colt. He looks to be an excellent young horse. That much I can tell from here. Boss said you done a fine job with the colt, seems to me he was right."

Blue stuck out his hand; "Name's Blue Mitchell." The Negro cocked his head; "I can see that, sir. My name is Willie Simms." Their grip was the same; despite Blue's height or the man's color, their hands were mutually strong, scarred, hardened from their years of work. There was no contest, no need for one; Blue suddenly recognized the name, knew why his face was familiar and was quick to acknowledge the man's reputation.

"It's the first time I met a real jockey, Mr. Simms. I've read about you and it is surely a pleasure." Simms dropped Blue's hand and stepped back; "You would not be funning me, Mr. Mitchell. I will not accept that treatment no more, Mr. Belmont he says I am the equal of any white rider. Yourself included, Mr. Mitchell."

They looked at each other, judging, and being judged, waiting for an opinion. Then Blue finished it; "You show me where you want the colt stabled and I'd be right appreciative if you'd lead us there. And no thank-you on the sights of the city, I ain't much for more'n two people at a time. I don't much like crowds, don't like most people. No offense, Mr. Simms."

Willie Simms laughed; "Mister Blue Mitchell even if your size let you, you'd never make the life of a jockey. Why the Queen herself has come up and congratulated me on a winning race. And when I rode Ben Brush. . ." His dark face smoothed, his smile grew and Blue found he too was grinning. "Mr. Mitchell there, we will get along just fine. There are a few people I truly respect, the rest are simply a matter of ignoring them." Blue had to laugh; the man spoke as Blue himself felt about the world.

The colt bolted out of the doorway, hitting the ramp only twice on his flight down from the cave where he'd been trapped. Blue laughed and held on to the last coils of the rope, acting as a weight to slow Curly's escape. The colt circled at the end of the rope, snorted, reared, came down kicking and Blue stood there, keeping a feel for the colt but not pulling or yanking, letting the youngster explore his body after a day or two of being shut up.

Simms stepped in close when the colt quit his antics. "He's a right lively youngster, now ain't he, Mister Mitchell." Blue only snorted and looked down onto the top of Willie's head. Never seen that kind of hair up close, looked like the man greased it down to keep it from rolling up tight; hell, here was Blue worrying about losing his hair, seeing all that gray in the dark blond strands – didn't matter, man's a man and each has his own vanity.

"What now, Mr. Simms?" Willie nodded, pointed to what Blue figured was north. "There's a track and small stalls there, 'bout a two mile walk. You up to that, mister cowboy? It seems I was told you started out with some bruised ribs."

Blue hesitated, wanted to see Willie's face and the man obligingly looked up. There was that glint, a slight turn to the mouth; "Now then, mister jockey, I guess if you can walk that distance, why I reckon a broke-down horse breaker like me can stagger along with you." The back and forth talk was pure foolishness and they both enjoyed it.

Curly was agreeable to the walk, long as he could step in next to Blue and keep a wary eye on the small fellow with the dark hands who walked quick and didn't talk much. That made for good company far as Blue was concerned.

It took less than a short hour, leaving Blue kind of wobbly in the knees, hell he hadn't walked this much since a good sorrel colt dumped him too many miles from the ranch headquarters. He'd hoped then he'd never have to walk this far in his slant-heeled boots, but Willie Simms and the colt marched along and by god and be damned Blue wasn't going to complain. Not in such important company.

There was a track ahead, fenced and smoothed, lined with seats on one side and long rows of stalls outside the fence.

Horses' heads popped out as they walked down one aisle, and the colt got all agitated and excited seeing so many of his kind. He was wanting to stand up and paw the air but Blue tugged, and talked, put a hand to the suddenly wet shoulder and the colt bounced down, shook his head and then shook all over and Blue laughed. It was mostly prancing and whinnying as they passed by all those possible new friends and Willie showed Blue a big stall, extra-sized, and separate from the others by one empty stall.

"No need to maybe spread a cough in either direction" was all Willie had to say. Blue's response was equally brief; "How long are we here?" Willie rubbed his head; "Mr. Belmont he thought two days plus today. Give the colt a workout and maybe you will let me ride him."

Blue did his own head scratching; "Now Mr. Simms I know your reputation and I understand Mr. Belmont he holds you in the highest regard. Seems to me we see alike on this one. It's only practical that maybe I'd ride Curly first, get some of the bounce out of him since I'm the only one's ever rode him. Hope that ain't an insult to you, sir, but this here colt's special and I aim to take the best care of him I can."

It became an odd moment; two men of unequal height and position in the outside world, sharing a skill and knowledge that few were privileged to claim. There was a brief flicker in Willie Simms' dark eyes, a retreat into insult that Blue watched and nodded to let him know. Then Simms relaxed, Blue almost laughed. "Mr. Mitchell." "Blue." "All right, Mr. Blue." Blue shook his head; "I ain't a mister, Mr. Simms. I'm a no 'count cowboy spent too much time with horses and kept away from people. Mister in any form don't set with me."

"Blue, did you bring any of your gear?" "I left it to the blacksmith in North Platte, had some doings with the man and Con, Mr. Norris I guess, he said I'd pick up a horse there to get me back to the ranch when this trip's done." "I take it the answer is no, then." Blue laughed; "I sure got to talking didn't I." Both men laughed and Curly stuck his head over the high half door, pushing against Blue's arm.

Simms brought them back to their business; "All I got here is flat saddles and a snaffle bit, we don't race or train in anything heavier. Mr. Belmont's gear is in New York, at the track, of course, but I can borrow something suitable. The training saddle we use, it's got some weight to it. Most cowboys they laugh at us for riding that gear but in a race. . ." "Willie, I ride my races on a blanket rolled up under my knees and I get laughed at but then again I usually win. So haul out one of those saddles and I'll give it a try. Who knows, I might find it a bit more comfortable than high withers and sweaty sides."

Willie shook his head; "You sure ain't what I thought a cowboy would be. Mr. Belmont he will be surprised."

NINE

It took maybe a half hour to get the light saddle on the restless colt. Blue eyed it, studied its design and remembered where he'd seen this saddle before, or one maybe like it. On the bay saddled by Joshua Snow and it was a damnable memory that had Blue shaking until he saw worry in the jockey's eyes. "I'm not used to steady ground yet." Simms nodded as if Blue had spoken the truth.

This saddle had little to it and yet Willie told him it was heavier than the standard race saddle. He felt a fool facing the saddle and its short stirrups hanging from thin leather straps, metal stirrups too far up for a decent-sized man to reach and he weren't asking for a hand up. Not from a man Willie's size. So he swung his body up on the colt's back, felt the chestnut shudder and take a quick step to accommodate Blue's sudden arrival. Blue slid right over the saddle and landed on his backside, sneezing as the dust rose around him, watching the colt's restless feet from the discomfort of the hard ground. Flat on his backside, he felt a complete fool. He glared up at Willie when he heard laughter.

Willie's dark hand reached down and offered Blue a pull. He thought to refuse it, then reckoned it too would be an insult. Willie pulled him up; Blue dusted off his britches and tried out a grin. "Looked a pure simpleton didn't I." Willie's face was set, his eyes wouldn't look at Blue. Ah hell, he thought, I've done insulted him.

The colt rubbed against Blue's arm. "Guess I'll try that mount up with a little less energy, didn't know I had it in me." He laughed and gathered up the reins, Willie stood at the colt's head, like he'd done on the first try, and Blue swung up and on this time, grabbing the saddle front and keeping himself close to the flat seat. The absurdly short stirrups and those leathers hung at his knees.

The colt spun and danced, pulled away from Willie and shook his head when Blue gathered the reins, drew his legs up and sat the colt's excitement. "Where to. . .?" He didn't have to finish; Willie pointed to a long alley of groomed sand, high fences, a closed gate that would open to the track. It looked like heaven to Blue, and obviously Curly had the same thoughts for it was easy directing him down the alley, going sideways most of the time but the colt was listening to Blue's hands, nodding his head, still traveling side to side but not rearing or bolting, which gave Blue time to find a toe hold in each stirrup. He stood, using his weight and height to bring the colt to a stop while Willie opened the gate.

Curly walked out onto the track, Blue hovering above him. It felt strange to be suspended over the horse's back but the empty openness of the place seemed to quiet Curly's excitement. The colt listened and for a few strides actually walked so Blue sat down, landing gently on the colt's back. Then as he touched the reins, he rose slightly, leaned forward and let the colt trot a few strides before sliding into a lope. The colt tugged and pulled, wanting more; Blue answered with a light hold, a soft releasing tug, saying no, keep to the easy lope.

The ground was gentle, cupping the colt's strides so that the beat of the lope was dispersed and cushioned without the heavy iron shoes. Blue'd never ridden such a course, not even the Army's track around the Fort Robinson field was this inviting.

He dropped a hand onto the colt's neck and swept his fingers across the chestnut hide, felt no heavy sweat or trembling; he was listening to the colt's breathing and it was unlabored. So he leaned forward, eased up on the reins, pressed his heels against the colt's sides and in two strides Curly was galloping. This was a ride Blue would never forget; there was nothing to fear, no trees or gullies or unseen holes, rocks or tree limbs. Just the pure heaven of good sand and an eager horse bred to run.

That mister Blue Mitchell could ride. Long legs bent impossibly into those high stirrups, calves and the inside of his heels light against the colt's sides, hands feeling the mouth, no fight, no resistance, just horse and rider wanting the same thing. Speed. Willie could feel every move, tasted the salt, felt the whip of the long mane against his hands and mouth.

Mr. Belmont he'd gone and bought himself a genuine racehorse.

Blue walked the colt for a good half hour after their run, two miles he reckoned, full speed and the colt was still hot, snorty and lathered but less on edge, more willing to listen. Willie offered to do the chore, said it was how he started on the race track, but Blue said he'd rode the colt into the lather, he'd do the walking.

With the colt dried and rubbed down, chewing on good hay in his extra large stall, Blue asked Willie Simms where they could get a meal, maybe a beer or two if Willie took a drink now and then. Willie shook his head; "Now you don't understand, do you? I can't go nowhere in this city with you where you'd want to eat. Those white-only places don't welcome my color. I can show you, Mr. Mitchell, but I can't walk through the front door and set down for the same meal with you."

Here truly was a world he'd never known. In his time he'd been thrown out of a bar or two, and off some ranches for questioning how the boss man handled the stock. But he'd never been judged openly for his color, well maybe as a kid his eyes and his own temper got him judged and juried without the facts, but this man knew exactly what folks saw when they looked at him, and it surely wasn't much to do with who he was.

There'd been buffalo soldiers at Fort Robinson but they were kept to themselves with a separate mess and white officers; it all was strange to Blue but it wasn't for him to question the Army, most of what they did was beyond his figuring.

He spoke the truth to Willie Simms; "Mr. Simms, whatever place you might have in mind to eat, I'd be honored to go with you, that is if they'll let a rounder like me in the place."

Willie looked up at his new companion. Mitchell was a tall lanky son, with heavy blond hair getting thinner on top, the long face dark-colored by the sun but nothing would ever make him a Negro. Especially the color of those eyes, a wild sea blue against startling whites; Willie bet the man did some fighting in his past over that arrogant stare. And he'd earned that arrogance around horses the hard way. Willie had seen the man ride, worked on the colt with him, and Willie judged those around him according to how they treated horses, and that had nothing to do with their color. He'd been treated almost that way in England and Europe. He could extend the same courtesy to Blue Mitchell here in Willie's home territory.

"I know a place serves good ribs and a fine pitcher of beer." Blue cocked his head, nodded, and Willie started out on a walk he'd rarely taken before. In Europe, with the Queen's approval, he was allowed in fine clubs and eating establishments, but only in the company of Mr. Belmont.

He glanced over at the loose-striding cowboy. The man could ride, Willie admired that, but he seemed to hold on to an innocence that had been beaten out of Willie years ago. Willie had raced against white men but never on an equal basis. They laughed at him, named his style of riding the monkey seat and called insults at him until he kept beating them while mounted on inferior horses and some of the braver men rethought their own riding style.

Now it was that supposed gentleman, Sloan, friend to the Prince of Wales and sweetheart to the English racing public, who rode the way Willie figured out, and Willie knew he was already forgotten.

This Mitchell, on the other hand, said he knew who Willie was and admired his way of racing. Told him the Indians rode that way, and that a time or two he'd rode on a blanket to lose the weight of the heavy stock saddle, and leaned forward to be with his horse. He won most races if he managed to stay on. Willie had a feeling this Mitchell didn't fall off his horse too often, that today's inelegant dismount had been a surprise.

He was curious as to the stock saddle and Mitchell explained it, how it had to be built strong enough to rope and tie or dally a seven-hundred pound steer wanting to get the hell and be gone from any human kind. Branding, doctoring, castrating; all those times a man needed a stout saddle and a sturdy horse. The flat saddle and Curly's long legs were useless to a cowhand.

But the lean build, the urge to run fast, was what made a good racehorse; Willie and this cowboy held that joy in common.

Willie chose a small place set on a corner, "Hattie's Bar" it was called, where women were allowed in to eat, with an escort, and the food was better'n most places he'd been. He hesitated, Mitchell ran into him. Leaned down, rested a hand on Willie's shoulder. His voice calm, slow, the words particularly soothing.

"Mr. Simms, I know I'll stick out like, well you know. But no man's going to keep me from a good meal. If you pick the place, then that's fine by me."

Willie crossed the littered floor, noticing the familiar crunch of peanut shells, hearing Blue follow him; then the place went dead quiet and Willie didn't like the feel of that silence. Some of the boys in here'd slice a white man's throat for a ragged silk kerchief.

Dark, smoke-filled, too many men cramped in a small place, hot scents of sweat and cook oils; the powerful odors turned Blue restless. Confined and no air, no sky; he almost turned back but his belly rumbled and he knew he'd never find his way to the track and the stall row and that empty stall where he'd thrown his gear.

Damn but it smelled good in here, right near a door looked like it went to a kitchen. Blue sat at a table near that door, figuring he'd get food quicker. Willie sat with him, shaking his head.

Willie made his observation, "Don't much set you off from your feed, does it." Here he had to stop, think, then saw Mitchell's eyes blazing to match that grin. He stood out like a lighthouse in this here bar. "Why some of these boys'd scalp you if they had the chance. Just for that pretty yellow hair."

Blue grinned again and in the dark room, with all the dark scowling faces, that white grin and the flash of those eyes told Willie the man could be pure trouble. Blue did make a promise though, and eased Willie's concerns. "I'll mind my manners long as someone feeds me soon enough."

Mitchell pushed back on the chair, leaned it to the wall, took off his hat and shook his head. That damnable blond hair swung free and loose, a mockery of those who sat near him. Even Willie, for that one moment, didn't much like the man. He had those looks got held up to every man of color, the long body, bright blue eyes, too-white teeth in the tanned face and the damnable blond hair. Ain't fair for one man to have it all and skill with the horses too.

A young woman, waist and skirt covered in a clean apron, approached them very carefully, holding out a small bit of cardboard. "We got this here food and what's on the wall, if you can read." She spoke to Willie but was staring at Blue like she was seeing a white man for the first time.

Blue put the chair on its four legs; "Miss, you tell me what's best and that's what I'll have. Maybe twice, if the food and I get along." For some unexplainable reason she giggled, and Blue grinned, and that made her laugh. Willie told her just one of those meals would do for him, and the girl walked away, shaking her head and still laughing.

Willie had a few minutes to study his companion, then he decided to hell with it, and asked; "You always have that way a getting a child woman to agree with you?" The question seemed to spark an old pain in Mitchell, for the eyes darkened, the mouth twitched, then with effort the man returned to his open and laughing self. "Willie, I say what comes to mind, and some women well they like being spoke to that way."

The meal appeared quickly, ribs and slaw, Blue eyed the vittles, took in the deep rich scent of spices he didn't recognize, but he was a brave man, had eaten snake and once thought seriously about a skunk, so what all the folks around him were enjoying he figured couldn't hurt him much. He raised his fork, took note of what lay where and went for the ribs.

Willie was picking up the ribs and chewing on them so Blue abandoned his attempt with the fork, a useless thing most of the time but women seemed taken with the supposed neatness they were meant to provide. It had taken some time but Blue stuck to it and learned how to handle the thing.

He pulled on the meat with his teeth, licked at the sauce, swallowed and felt some better. Belly wasn't so angry with him now it had something else to work on. He looked at Willie, who was chewing sideways at a whole new angle and Blue admired the man's technique.

He had a few comments and questions as they worked through the food; "Could use some chile to it but man this is good, what're these small things, I ain't used to much beyond steak and a few spuds, beans mostly, and canned peaches.

Had lettuce once, in a lady's house." His eyes shifted again and Willie guessed the memory wasn't all as sweet or shallow as it sounded.

"That's rice, Blue. And here, shake on some of this hot sauce, that'll outdo your chile any time." He winced as Blue smothered the rice in red sauce and as he watched, he admired the man; sweat soaked his forehead and his eyes turned a hotter blue but he ate every last bit and asked the girl for that second helping. Guess that chile the man spoke of had its own brand of heat. Willie was impressed.

Four men stood up and followed at a brief distance when Blue and Willie left the saloon. Willie looked back once and the biggest man was using a glistening knife to clean his fingernails. Willie cocked his head to Blue, who spoke out loud, too loud, in answer to Willie's unsaid warning.

"Hell I got me a knife 'bout that size, maybe a bit smaller, does the job though. And I'm right handy with it, better'n a gun, can get in close and feel the flesh give way. Makes a man proud he can cut 'nother son of a bitch like that. It's sure as hell more personal than using a bullet to step back and shoot." Willie jerked his step at the words, and unexpectedly the four men stopped, stood outside near the doorway as Blue wandered down the street, headed by pure instinct toward the barn.

Willie hurried, Blue slowed down to get them back in step. He was almost laughing; "Those rannies didn't have manners, Willie. So I figured to speak up, but I sure didn't expect they'd believe me." Willie studied on the facts a moment; "Then you don't have a knife." "Hell, Willie, I'm good for riding horses and that's about it. Got in enough trouble though I learned a few words set most men back on their haunches. And half the time if I speak up I get out of the fight coming at me. I know I look like a mad man, and there ain't nothing I can do 'bout that."

Willie'd never known a man who saw himself like this one, with a confidence from a lot of years of fights, arguments, wounds and hurts. For whatever reason, this Mitchell chose to keep to the life, content when he had a horse to work, miserable among people. Any type of people, Willie decided, black or white. Most likely he got 'long with them Indians though, he'd already spoke of racing them, learning there to ride hunched over the horse's back.

The next morning Blue saddled Curly and let him loaf around the track, then headed over to Willie. "Here, you try him, he pulls to the right but listens pretty good." They had to draw up the stirrups five holes, and Willie accepted a leg up.

Riding the chestnut colt was a pleasure. The horse listened to the bit, the rider's commands and thoughts, tugging, veering to the right as he'd been warned but willing to accept Willie's suggestion that he run the middle of the course.

"Let him go!" Blue's voice, excited, demanding; "I've never seen him run." Blue let out a sigh and watched.

Traveling again in the boxcar was rough after the freedom of that good track and the taste of decent food. He even considered he might have made a friend in Willie Simms, and Blue took friendship hard for it wasn't his nature to trust.

Watching Curly run had been the best. Blue leaned his head on the stall slats and the colt reached over, tugged at his hair then went back to eating hay as if he'd earned the right. Seeing that colt run with a good rider was a treat Blue savored. He could understand how Willie won so many races against the odds. Perched almost above the horse, small frame rolled up out of the way, hands liquid on the bridle reins; the colt fought him once, reared and plunged and Willie's small body went with him, was there when the colt came down, hands still soft, never turning hard even while asking for the colt to quit fussing and run.

Blue'd spent the night comfortably in the extra stall, content with the noise and smell of horses, always the best part of his life. Willie woke him in the morning with a cup of coffee, told him there was eggs and ham cooked over a short fire at the far end of the shedrow and he was welcome to eat there.

Willie didn't wait but told Blue that Mr. Belmont he had Willie booked on a train East, leaving in an hour, he'd see him in New York, it'd been a pleasure riding on that chestnut colt.

The men doing the cooking were the varying shades of dark that Blue was beginning to understand. Like the buffalo soldiers at Fort Robinson, they were polite to him but held him in little esteem. He reckoned but for Willie's speaking up on him, these men would have denied him food and simply stared back at whatever he asked.

They filled a plate, one man pointed to the coffee pot hissing to the side of the fire, and then they went back to their talk of horses and odds and whose best prospect had broken down and how long it would take to mend.

Blue ate standing, back against the warmth of a stall, a horse put his head out over the half door to keep Blue company so he talked to the horse while he ate. The food was decent cooked, it needed chile or that hot sauce but Blue was getting used to the neglected fact.

The horse seemed interested as Blue described his journey, starting with the wolf and then the son of a bitch who'd tried to steal the chestnut colt. And he even talked some on Rhynes; man who found his true heart when he got pushed to the wall. That's how a man learned about himself, Blue told the horse, while he himself chewed over the eggs and toasted bread. A man didn't know his own heart until life got bad and he had choices to make.

It had been good timing for Blue when Rhynes found his soul, Blue told the companionable bay head; if Rhynes had backed off, there'd be one dead horse breaker and a missing chestnut colt and he and the bay wouldn't be having this particular conversation.

He realized that very slowly the band of men had stopped their own jabbering and were listening to his elaborated tale;

mostly the truth, just a few things maybe enlarged some to make a point.

Blue grinned at the men as he returned the plate; "Thanks for sharing, fellas, guess I got me a colt to load and a ways to travel."

He didn't look back, just walked his own steps back down the shedrow where he spent time getting Curly ready for his continuing education in the ways of a famous race horse.

Loading onto the boxcar and settling in was a simple matter this time; Curly stood at the base of the ramp, lowered his head and sniffed the swept wood planks, then raised his head and pushed out his upper lip. Something on the wood was familiar to him. Then he stepped up the ramp as if he'd done nothing but this loading and unloading his whole life.

After a short ride in the rocking, jerking car, Blue began to smell something out of place; with the colt watching him over the stall gate, he poked around until he found a canvas sack that smelled familiar. Even as he opened the sack he was grinning; hell, Willie did it to him. Caught him by surprise. Inside, wrapped in thick paper, was more of that food, spilled over with red sauce, ribs with a sweetness that melted away as he chewed.

For Blue, the memory of Chicago would remain mostly tastes and smells of different food, his hand being accepted by Willie Simms, and watching the chestnut colt run.

TEN

He and the colt finally got used to the rhythm again, the sway of their temporary home, the stops and starts where they automatically braced again a wall. Blue found the motion of the train made him constantly sleepy, and eventually he noticed the colt dozing, head low, knees locked, ears loose. Finally the colt would lie down, resting in the deep bedding with his nose propped on the padded floor.

Blue never even saw New York City; the train went on through to the Brighton Race Track on Coney Island. Leastways that's what he learned later. He was asleep when they passed by the city and when someone said, 'What, you missed New York', Blue answered that it was another pile of houses and too many people and he didn't see what was so great about the place.

When the boxcar door finally slid open, Blue and the colt were more than willing to walk on steady ground. Four men drew out the ramp, then a man in neat clothes appeared, carrying a leather halter and plaited lead, nodding vaguely to Blue as he approached the stalled colt.

Blue stepped between the man and his intended victim. "Mister, you talk to me first. I ain't come all this distance to let just any son walk up to my colt and take him."

"Your colt?" A voice behind the first man demanded his attention; damn he hadn't registered the second set of steps up that ramp. Blue took a side step and stared at the newcomer. Another neat and tidy man, hair slicked back, a plain face with a graying mustache to hide his mouth. Right had been trying to grow one of those bushes under his nose, kept coming out a red color that Right didn't like much, and it got in his food, he said, made the stew taste of whiskers and hay and anything else he picked up during a day's work.

This man, he must have figured out how to tame a mustache, and he wore one of those hard collars Blue'd read about, tight enough around his neck so that a roll of flesh hung over its edge. Two dandies in one day, both of them wanting the colt.

Blue moved back to the colt's stall and of course the chestnut head popped over the barred doorway, the muzzle pushed against Blue's arm and he let his fingers play with the colt's whiskers.

"Gentlemen." He watched both of them as he spoke; "One of you give me papers or reasons why you come hunting this colt, why then I'll look 'em over and let you know what I think. Till then, this colt and me, we stay right here."

He'd been told about this man, in a neatly worded telegram sent by Willie that reached him this morning. He eyed the rough-hewn gentleman from the western plains, trying to reconcile what he saw with what his agent and his jockey had told him.

True, those eyes were most unusual, and the ragged, rather dirty hair was blond, although laced with gray, which tended to give an estimate of the man's age. While he was lean, and tall enough, he was no longer a boy but a man well into his thirties and showing the effects of his rough years.

Despite what the man's appearance indicated, Willie had been highly excited about Mitchell's skill with the colt, and bragged on the colt itself, briefly mentioning that in Chicago they had both ridden the colt on the track there, and Willie was of the opinion that Mr. Belmont had bought himself a winner.

Willie's train had arrived early this morning, and he'd been given orders to sleep, clean himself up, take a day to settle back in before coming to the track. Belmont himself would deal with Mr. Mitchell; he wanted to meet the man without Willie at his side to change the first impression.

August Belmont cleared his throat, the man holding the halter backed up until he stood just at Belmont's shoulder, slightly behind him.

"I am indeed the owner of this colt, Mr. Mitchell. Willie Simms told me you would be protective of him. Here, my bill of sale from Mr. Norris should make you rest easy and allow me to take possession of my new horse."

The cowhand stepped forward, hands at his side but a grin starting; "Hell, mister. You're Belmont himself." Belmont nodded; "Yes, and this is my assistant trainer, George Bowdry. Do you still need to see the papers giving me authority to retrieve my own colt?"

Belmont knew he would like the man, even as his agent and Willie trusted him for his protective instincts. Mitchell wasn't ready to turn the horse over yet. "Mr. Belmont, now I've read about you, and I heard folks talk about you and your horses, and your famous papa, and you wanting to put folks underground in what they call subways, but I ain't never seen a picture of you looks much like a person, and while I can guess, I can't be sure till I see something down in writing, that an ignorant son like me can read mind you."

August smiled and nodded, pleased with the man's stubbornness. In the racing world, such a ploy as to take by connivance a man's good horse was not unheard of and he was delighted to know that Mr. Norris had indeed sent along his best.

"Here, Mr. Mitchell, here's the telegraph Willie sent, which speaks highly of you and your ride at the track. And here also is my bill of sale for this colt, what do you call him? Brush Fire is a fine name for racing, but what is he called around the stables?"

Blue snorted, took the papers and studied them, even held the telegraph form up to the light. He'd never seen such before, though the words themselves were an easy enough read. But the bill of sale was enough; he knew Con Norris's sign. The words in Willie's telegraph made him uncomfortable.

"All right, Mr. Belmont, let me halter and take this boy out. He ain't use to most folks touching him. Before this trip I'm the only one rode him. Con tried playing with him one day and got his ankle and a wrist busted for the fun." He nodded to the assistant trainer, one George Bowdry, and bent down to pick up the coiled rope and crude halter. "We called him Curly, he's got that whirl on his forehead and one on his neck. I read it as temper and thinking, most horses got that whirl can be sons a bitches but they're smart."

He'd thought about trying to talk proper or keep his mouth shut, but this man bought a horse, nothing more than that. And if his face in the paper made him famous, and he spent his money on racehorses, then he'd heard everything there was to say about the contrariness of the animals.

Done talking, gathering the rope, Blue glanced up and noted that Belmont was watching silently as his assistant went back down the ramp in a manner said his temper and assumed importance had been insulted.

Curly was sure eager to get out of his stall; the trip'd been too long for anything brought up on range distance and the smell of good air, heat and cold, tall grass and clear water. Ah hell, Blue thought, I'm talking 'bout myself mostly. The horse was bred to run, and if that's what he was going to do, then he'd come home.

Curly knew the ramp now, and for once he walked down its slippery wood proper, keeping his muzzle firmly planted on Blue's arm. They'd landed in horse heaven; horses everywhere, in longer shedrows, heads poked out to stare at the newcomer.

The colt stopped, reared, Blue let the rope lengthen until he tugged gently on the line, the colt came down, snorted slobber all over Blue's face and chest. He laughed and slapped the colt's chest. "You act right, Curly, this here's your new life."

Mr. Bowdry led the way to a single row of stalls. Blue noted the stall doors were painted all the same color, with a B in the middle – so the rich man had himself his own private kingdom. He thought of Con's kingdom, land and grass and distance where a man could lose himself, and he shook his head. This sure wasn't going to become his home. Belmont however seemed to have differing ideas on the subject, and Blue got the distinct impression that most folks did exactly as Belmont said.

Man couldn't know yet that Blue did what he chose to do, following orders wasn't in his nature.

"Mr. Mitchell, Mr. Norris has given his permission that you remain a few weeks to help the colt settle in. Willie is looking forward to riding him again, but I would like to see you work with him. Mr. Bowdry here thinks at times I am perhaps a bit too fond of my animals, but they are such honest beasts, a true rarity in my largely commercial world."

August Belmont wondered as he listened to his own words, why he spoke so openly with a stranger, one whose life had no connection to him other than a universal concern for horses, and an obvious and highly marketable talent with these fractious beasts.

Blue shrugged. "It makes no mind to me, you got a stall here, I can sleep in comfort." Belmont chose to argue, and the look on Bowdry's face told Blue he'd not ever come to like the man. There was a sneer dug into Bowdry's features, hard lines at his mouth come down from his nose; nothing would make this man laugh or change his mind.

Belmont insisted; "Mr. Mitchell, there are hotels where our staff stay through the meets. I cannot allow. . ." Here he became cautious since he knew something of the western temperament. "Only the grooms live in the shedrows with their horses, and they are. . .well they are Negroes." To his consternation, Mitchell grinned and Belmont had the unnatural feel of wanting to hit a man he barely knew.

"I ain't had a good history in hotels, Mr. Belmont. I've been thrown out of enough of them, too many people in too small a space for my tastes. I know Willie and you say he sleeps here, well that's good enough for me. 'Least I got a friend or two with him and Curly." It was settled, Blue would sleep in one of the stalls.

There was silence, no motion even from the colt, and it gave Blue a chance to look where he'd landed this time. He wasn't much taken with the place but still curious. Horses, stalls, piles of steaming manure, a series of towers, seats that went up in layers to the towers, motor cars and a train that ran from overhead wires. A whole city built up around horses and water. He saw it then, a long distance of blue, small white tops, a smell like he'd never know. And the sound, a constant push and slap, easy on the ears, making him stand quiet and watch.

Belmont came up to him then, interrupting a vision Blue was enjoying; "There still is a question, Mr. Mitchell. Where will you take your meals? You cannot cook here at the shedrow, and Willie eats at a. . ." There was that polite wait again, as if a certain word wasn't spoke proper by a gentleman. Blue shook his head; "Hell, Mr. Belmont, me and Willie we had a fine meal in Chicago and no one there gave us trouble. A couple of the boys followed us outside but we talked about knives and where it hurt most to cut a man and those boys kind of disappeared."

Belmont made sure he was looking straight into Mitchell's face. No doubt of it, the man was teasing him a bit, overstating the evening's meal but still telling him that Willie's color, and Mitchell's own coloring for that matter, made no difference to either man.

"That is fine then with me, Mr. Mitchell. I will set it up at the local café, your name and that you work for me, your meals are to be on my tab, as I do with Willie. It is only fair, since I cannot force you to accept the finer accommodations in one of our hotels."

He hesitated while studying the man standing so loose and easy before him, holding the chestnut colt who kept nudging at Mitchell's arm or shoulder, obviously eager to see his new home but mindful of the manners Mitchell had taught him. "I have a feeling, sir, that you have rightfully declined the hotel offer. I would dislike having to bail you out of our local law enforcement establishment."

Belmont then rubbed his chin very slowly; "I don't usually come to the track, Mr. Mitchell, to see to the arrival of a new acquisition. It is Mr. Bowdry who tends to such detail. I would like you to understand that Mr. Bowdry has my full authority."

There seemed to be a series of hesitations in Belmont's statement. Blue watched Bowdry, who looked to grow taller with the unintended praise. Then Blue glanced away, at the masses of people, the noise and clang of cars and business. He returned to study the dapper gentleman in front of him.

"Mr. Belmont, I usually ride horses, or run them, not nurse them on a train ride. Guess we're 'bout even on what we do and don't do."

Blue had the distinct feeling that Mr. August Belmont Jr. might have learned a thing or two about getting along. And from a broke-down cowhand, a man who could cause a fight just by saying howdy to a pretty woman.

Blue made sure Curly was settled in a big stall at the end of the row, with plenty of good hay and clean water. He spent some time going through the hay, picking out stalks and sniffing them before deciding that Belmont's riches bought damned fine feed. It'd do to keep the colt in good flesh.

Blue promised the colt he'd come back for a run and then a grooming, but he needed to get his gear off the box car 'fore it disappeared. He told the two men of his intent, paying no attention to what their faces said in return. He was restless and needed to move, get going, too bad there wasn't a good cow horse for him to jump on and ride, a good run chasing a muley steer, but this time walking would have to do.

"Think I'll take me a look see, Mr. Belmont, Mr. Bowdry, I ain't never been near water like this before." He nodded to the men and backtracked to the box car, got out his gear and put it in an open stall near to Curly's new home, then started along a road next to a track that had those overhead wires. More'n likely they'd bring him someplace close to the water. The ocean; he knew what it was from reading. But he sure as hell never thought to see it.

ELEVEN

Belmont and Bowdry watched the long-legged cowboy walk away. It was a study in loose locomotion; legs and arms and that easy way of moving against the beach sand, with a slight limp, then up on the rail bed. High heeled boots and that hat made the man a sight to see on the boardwalk.

Belmont had to keep in mind what Con Norris had told him about Blue Mitchell, while George Bowdry hoped some of

92

the street bums found the man and beat him half senseless. He didn't like or trust anyone with that much confidence and he already disliked how quickly Mr. Belmont responded to the man's rough charm. That colt, well, it might be able to run but it was range-broke, and would find the lights and sounds of a big-time racetrack far too much for its undisciplined mind.

He planned to be nearby when Mitchell was aboard the colt in the highly predictable runaway.

August Belmont smiled to himself; he could feel the waves coming off Bowdry, who was excellent as an assistant in charge of scheduling the races, keeping track of the winnings, the losses, ordering bedding and finding the best hay; all the practical and mathematical shenanigans that were attendant upon a successful racing stable.

When he had fired Horace Danforth, it had been unsaid but alive between them that Bowdry wanted the head trainer position. It would not do, Belmont was too aware of Bowdry's consistent failings where the actual horses were concerned. He had made an effort, raised the man's salary and spoke highly of the man's organizational talents, but it would never be enough to buy the prestige of being known as August Belmont, Jr.'s head trainer.

That title, and the daily pressure of correct decisions, now belonged to Mr. Edward Franklin, recently departed from the Dwyer Stable after suspicion was high in a race where none of the horses ran true to form. Belmont had removed himself from the discussion and had no qualms on hiring Mr. Franklin as being untainted by the scandal. The Dwyer brothers, whether they worked together or were on the outs with each other, could be counted on to be indiscreet and greedy in their racing strategy.

Franklin would begin his position in a month's time; he had family commitments, which August accepted as part of the employment terms. He did insist, however, that Franklin meet with Bowdry and explain in detail his training schedule for each horse. It was Franklin's methodical and practical approach to the horses that August particularly admired. His willingness to allow each horse its own personality pleased him, for what August had realized early in his life around horses, at his father's side, was that horses indeed were living beings and not simply items with which adult males indulged their need to own the best.

Bowdry's reception to Franklin's power had been a lesson in diplomacy or its lack thereof and the uncomfortable consequences. It was on August's mind to fire the man, but so far Bowdry had redeemed his bout of sulking by higher-than-usual standards of procurement and adherence to the particulars of Franklin's' regime. August believed fully in the effects of good food, clean water, and well-mannered stable help to relax his horses and allow them to tend to their vocation, which was to run in his silks and win races in his name.

With men and animals, Bowdry was less than successful. Which meant that the head trainer, Edward Franklin, would take over from Mitchell after the man was allowed his turn on the track. It was only from what Willie Simms had to say that Belmont would consider such a breach of training policies. But he wanted to watch the cowboy ride. And it meant keeping the man here for the intervening month until Franklin reappeared just in time for the Futurity at Sheepshead Bay.

Damn it was hot; he felt sweat pouring down his back, soaking his pants, stinking up what was left of his shirt and his pride. These folks were crazy to cram themselves into these motorbuses and cars and come together in crowds to walk too close along board walkways laid over hot sand. And then tell themselves they was some cooler for the walking and parading and not getting their feet wet. It was a fool business.

The sand was familiar. He stopped, lost already, nothing else around him familiar or comfortable; no horses, good grass, a cottonwood tree, the Pecos or Carizzo River, a pronghorn bouncing ahead of him, spooking the untried colt he was riding.

It was all these people, dressed in those fancy high collars, the ladies with long skirts and carrying a shell over their head to keep off the sun. It was summer, July or maybe early August, and he knew the cities would be hot and damn near unbearable. So these folks came to the ocean, dressed in their finery and walked up and down in the heat, sweating and uncomfortable like he was.

Where was the damned ocean, and why weren't all these proper fools sticking their feet in the water or swimming in the cold? He'd learned quick as a boy how to swim, never wore nothing, which couldn't be done with so many folks watching, but he could step in the water and cool his feet.

Walking on the wood, or the hard sidewalk, was hell on a man's feet, nevermind the rest of him.

He stood quiet, let folks split and go around him Blue raised his head, listened, turned his face and sniffed, felt the wind on his face, inhaled and tasted salt. The ocean had to be close by since that smell couldn't travel too far against the heated engines and food cooking, the human mass.

Ocean water, salted like he'd been told it was, something he didn't believe until now he could smell it. He had to taste, see, maybe stick a toe in and come to an understanding.

Another half hour and he was losing his focus; folks stared, a bunch of kids followed him for a while, pointing and laughing. Hell he knew he was out of place and paid them no mind till they got bored and went on to torment other targets.

Then he crossed a street that had a sign on a pole and an arrow pointing so he went where he was told. Damned unusual for him to follow directions but it was better than more aimless walking.

There it was, a long hill of sand, a flatness that slanted to heavy water rolling back and out, wetting the sand, then scuttling away and coiling up into itself as if fearful before charging in again.

He marched deliberately up and over the hill, regretting those boots but they were what he had. Guess he hadn't had time to pack his swimming garments, whatever was in fashion this year. He'd seen the pictures, men in flat hats and wool knickers and women wearing ruffles and high stockings under more ruffles.

Blue grinned as he stepped onto the sand. Cool air snuck into his lungs and he sighed, coughed, spat out dust and distance.

A few people were actually walking on the hard beach; men mostly, wearing outlandish outfits and those flat straw hats that made them look a fool to a cowboy's more practical eye.

One man detached himself from a group and walked, or rather marched, into the water, being hit continually by rolling curls. Eventually he leaned forward against a particular slap and disappeared into the high-thrown water. He reappeared only a few minutes later – too long Blue thought, but the man bounced up and waved at his companions.

There weren't ladies on the beach, at least not in those outfits, which, Blue decided was smart since a man would see too much, especially when that woman got herself wet.

That fellow coming out of the water wasn't too modest with what he was showing either; wool suit or not, a man kept some things to himself.

The idea of getting into that water was appealing, and Blue didn't need to stand downwind of himself to smell his stink. Since no one mentioned a bath at the barns, and there was only a hand pump and little privacy, he guessed dousing himself in the ocean was good as anything else to hand for scrubbing himself clean.

He sat, pulled at a boot, emptied out a private bucketful of Nebraska soil mixed with New York sand, stripped off the sock, held it away from him and figured he'd best take it in the water, the other one too as he removed the other boot.

Looking back as he got near the water, there stood his boots, simple brown leather, cracked and patched along the outside of the foot, toes curled up, heel rotting but still useable. Not much and all he had.

Laughing, he stepped into the rolling water, flinched from the cold, a surprise to him on such a sunny, damned hot day. He never thought that water could be so downright miserable. Hell, he'd take Yellowstone in mid-winter to this chill. 'Course it was the hot springs that made the waters in Wyoming possible in the snow, and there sure weren't no hot springs here.

Another curl, a splash high on his chest made him think again about pushing into the water full blast like the well-dressed man had done. That wave gave Blue a full appreciation for the man's internal courage.

Then he stepped in deeper, trying to catch up to the leaving water, got slapped by its return in places that shrunk back and he wanted to cross his hands, hold on, warm up some; instead he jumped in, face forward, arms flailing, and skidded on sand, damn that water left a man stranded right quick.

Sand scraped his chin, the palms of his hands, and he rolled over, felt a new wave lift him, drag him out into the water, sand attacking his neck. He laughed as he was rolled, then he got to his knees, his feet froze to the wet sand; he thought, damn the water was cold.

He walked out to the retreating water, breasting the water's return assault, he was too conscious of wet clothes clinging to him but the water felt good, cooling him down, maybe not sweetening his disposition but definitely improving the air around him.

Being back on dry sand and civilization, wet hair hanging in his eyes, mouth and fingers burning, lips chapped, ears tickled with water, Blue felt alive. He wished he could shuck off his clothes and roll back into the water, but now there was a group, several of them, standing too close together, watching, talking, waving their hands in his direction so he couldn't miss their message. Making him feel the fool he most likely was in their eyes.

But damn he'd been swimming in the ocean. It was one hell of a thing for a Nebraska or Colorado, Wyoming or New Mexico cowboy to say to himself, so he repeated the words out loud, complete with the swearing, and several of the congregating folks stepped back, even let their eyes widen. Guess no one in the East swore much or talked out loud with his thoughts to himself. Then again they always had another human nearby to listen. A man couldn't talk to himself or his horse, if he had one, in private here. Too damned crowded and he wanted to tell the growing crowd exactly what he thought.

Couldn't do that, get in a fight first day he was in town. For that would be the reaction to what he wanted to say.

Blue nodded to one particular group, then turned away from them, sat down to let himself dry, then get the sand off his feet so he could get into the tight stinking boots and walk back, he hoped, to the racetrack. He'd be hot all over again by the time he got there, but right now he felt clean.

He walked up onto the boards, drew in a quick breath, let it out and started toward the track. He felt a bump, heard a kid's yell, looked up and there she was. Older, prettier, eyes soft, a muted cry as her hand rose to her mouth. Then she reached toward him, took the child who'd run into him, held the boy close.

Blue turned brittle and unbelieving. The child looked up at him, vivid blue eyes wide open, blond hair curled around his face. "You're a cowboy. A real one, I know that." The voice was small and young, a child's voice filled with grown-up ideas.

TWELVE

"Ma'am." He managed to yank off his hat, bowed his head, heard a ringing in his ears and his feet got too far away from him. Knowing folks had to be staring at his outrageous clothing and actions against the woman's soft beauty and the child's remarkable appearance. The air got thick, his hands tingled, he was conscious of his own body. The kid looked at him; "You're all wet. Cowboys don't go in the water."

Blue's heart lurched in his chest as he reached out and touched the boy's hair, looked over him to his mother. "How old?" She nodded; "Eight years and five months." She nodded again; spoke very softly. "Yes." The single word robbed his mind.

Her voice was very pleasant, and quite distant, as if his appearance did not disturb her. "It is nice to see you, Mr. Mitchell." Then she finished him off; "I hope we meet again soon. Come along now, Robert."

She turned the child, who obviously wanted to stay and examine this peculiar man who seemed to know his mother. She pushed him in small motions until he had to walk, although he could turn his head and stare back at the man, who stood there, motionless on the boardwalk, wet hair drying in tangled spikes, bright blue eyes sparkling like they were still wet.

He needed to ask his mother who the man was, why hadn't he said his name to them, but she leaned down gently, put two fingers on his mouth and said 'shush' which meant he was talking too much and his papa would be annoyed but Papa wasn't anywhere in sight and Robert wanted to know exactly who the man was.

A dark face stopped Blue; not a familiar face but one that looked worried. "Mister, you all right? They don't 'llow drunks on this here street, the police they keep an eye out for the drinkers, this being a family place and all. I were you, mister, I'd find a hole and set there a spell till it gets dark night or you sober up some."

The words were senseless until Blue shook his head and realized he was half in the road, half on that damnable board walkway and about ready to set down. He studied the black face, noted it was darker than Willie Simms but there was kindness in the burnt eyes.

"Mister." He tipped the front of his hat. "I sure would 'preciate it you show me where that racecourse went and hid."

The man smiled, white teeth against dark skin still a shock to Blue. "Mister cowboy, now I know you ain't drunk, just got yourself lost and don't know how to get on home. Word's gone out on you from Willie, to keep a watch. Can't have no cowboy lost in Brighton Beach. Not among these folks with their high-toned ways."

Blue thought the man's words were too close to the truth but he needed guidance, and took note of the pointed finger, the few words, mumbling left and right, a tall post, a street sign and then he'd smell the manure and know where he was.

Blue thanked the man, no names exchanged, yet as he turned to start in a new direction, his rescuer said; "Say hi to ole Willie from Walker down to Rory's Tavern. You tell him now."

As if he were drunk, his feet couldn't find a straight line, his body rebelled, hands nerveless, eyes aching from what he'd seen. His boy, that hair came from his own ma, those eyes belonged to him, the face was hers, a sweetness and beauty Blue knew wasn't in him.

Hell and be damned, he truly was a father. The older boy, Joshua, said he was, told him where they lived. Blue had tried hard not to think, dared not to guess this might happen. But he knew, admitted only to himself, that the hope was why he didn't fight Con on making the trip, or Belmont on having him stay a few weeks. He had tried not to, wouldn't imagine what it would be like. . .his own son.

He ached to touch the child. She had said it, though, 'I hope to see you again, Mr. Mitchell. Soon.' She said it to him. That had to mean something but he couldn't find her, didn't know her last name. She wasn't Dorothy Snow, not the woman he'd known. The boy's name was Robert, he was sure he'd heard her say the name. Or was it in his mind where he'd told her his true given name. He didn't tell people his name, no one. Yet his, their son, was named Robert.

He struggled with the name, the vision; he didn't remember telling her but he'd been pretty damned sick to her house, what he might of said wouldn't stay with him. Fever did that to a man. Could she have known so soon he would be that important?

No decent woman would take up with a man like Blue; yet he remembered her cries of pleasure and then a sad, gentle remorse. Her sweetness was a rarity to him, was it possible she had felt the same way. He could not ever believe that a woman of Dorothy Snow's breeding and education could love a drifter, not even for one perfect night.

The shedrow and manure piles were blessed; Blue began to feel his feet again, his hands were his own and his mouth worked. His mind was still with her, but the horses, their familiar sounds, would be quick to save him.

She was a woman he'd known once, lived in her house, was tended by her, came to know her, then love her. It was wrong for she had a husband. Had a husband now, from what he'd been told. His own ma had taught him better, about honor and keeping a man's given word.

The sharp pain was worse than any wound, broke ribs or busted leg, the bullet high in his chest, all those were nothing compared to memorizing the boy's face, hearing the mother's soft voice.

A shape stepped out from a stall; "You's here, Mr. Mitchell." Blue coughed, wiped his mouth, hitched up his sagging pants. Willie Simms had no knowing of Blue's fancies; the man grinned, figuring Blue'd come back to ride. "That colt's settling in right well, Mr. Belmont he thinks Mr. Norris done him well. Said he'd like you to take the colt out, not under saddle but walking maybe, let him stretch his legs and see his new home."

Blue nodded, mouth too goddamn dry to speak. Briefly he heard Con's voice in the swearing. For that moment, he felt safe.

Blue walked past Willie, baring his teeth in pretending to smile, hoping the man wouldn't know the difference. The colt came to the stall front hearing Blue's cracked voice. 'Curly.' That's all it took; he got nuzzled and picked on and then the colt washed his face, chin, nose, cheek and Blue had to laugh. Hell, he was a walking salt lick.

A halter and short lead got handed to Blue and the colt pushed his head into the contraption, eager to get out and get moving. Curly danced sideways, snorting, shaking his head and never quite coming to the end of the lead, never yanking or bullying his friend, just rowdy enough to let Blue know; Curly hadn't liked living in a stall and was eager to show his displeasure.

Simms came with them, walking to Blue's left, away from the jigging colt. They got out into the sun, heavy heat, no wind, nothing but sand track, white fence, too many stalls with horses, no one on the course.

Blue gestured and Willie opened the gate to the track. The man knew, understood – a good horse, a fast track, no one and nothing else mattered.

Blue tied the lead around Curly's neck to the off side of the halter and swung up on the already steaming hide. Nobody was watching, no one cared. He looked down at Simms, whose dark face was closed, the eyes barely looking at him. The voice was soft but carried its own authority; "Mr. Belmont he said nothing 'bout you riding today, just take the colt for a walk."

"Willie, it's my choice, I ain't fit for walking Curly like a pet dog. Hell, he's a runner, I plan to let him run. Nothing here can hurt him 'cepting my stupidity if I fall off. And hell, he said not under saddle and I'm up here like a fool with nothing but hide and hair to keep me in place."

George Bowdry stood in the small office Mr. Belmont had built for his valued staff. He watched the foolishness going on at the track, and smiled. Here was his ammunition; Mr. Belmont gave the orders, not a no-account cowboy who had no manners or understanding. Mr. Belmont would not be pleased.

The black and white feist that kept Bowdry company on those days he had to work at the track jumped up with its front paws on the window ledge. The dog barked once, Bowdry raised his hand and the feist was silent; tail down, ears flat, but still watching the running horse.

Bowdry kept his vigil, the feist remained with him, knowing only that its job was to stay beside its master.

It would too soon become Mr. Franklin's orders, Mr. Franklin allowing this outlandish and undisciplined rider to run a young horse at high speeds, thereby ruining the pattern of the training Mr. Franklin outlined for the owner, Mr. Belmont. That Franklin had not yet met the colt, or its rider, meant nothing. There would be a plan, and Bowdry would see that the training regime would be of primary importance in breaking the chestnut colt to the racetrack's ways.

The bigger affront was to Mr. Belmont's reputation more than anything else; the unregulated manner in which the cowboy handled the colt. Right now, riding without benefit of saddle or bridle, loose hair flying, knees drawn up in that ungainly and undignified seat that Belmont insisted upon but was often mocked by other trainers and owners; there he was, flying around the track on a badly disciplined animal, putting Mr. Belmont's reputation for dignity and honor to shame.

This was not acceptable to George Bowdry; the cowboy had to be stopped before his unruly behavior affected the rest of the stable crew.

If the colt had the required speed, and that was still to be determined, and was willing enough to allow other riders to direct it, then would come the test of actually racing against other horses of equal speed and far better breeding, in the vivid carnival atmosphere of an organized race meet.

This unwarranted display of impulse would be explained both to Mr. Franklin and Mr. Belmont at the proper time. When the colt's failure to win would become the topic of heated conversation.

The feist barked again, and jumped away from the windowsill as Bowdry's boot sought to kick the small dog in the ribs as a reminder. Bowdry did not like barking dogs.

Most of the stable hands drifted to the fence rail, stood in quiet groups, a rake or shovel in hand, readied to spring back into working but they wanted to watch, to see and understand what Willie had been telling them.

It was quickly agreed that Mitchell could ride. No saddle or cloth, no stirrups, not even a decent leather rein and bit. Just a thin, finely stitched leather halter and a braided lead to steady the colt's head as he moved in easy strides that lengthened into a full-blown run and each man sighed, knowing he would bet on this one to win wherever he ran. 'Less some vandal or hoodlum got to the colt and nobbled him.

They went back to work in small movements just as the chestnut colt slowed his burst of speed, responding to the light tugs of the wild man riding him.

The colt had wanted to run, Blue felt it with every quiver of the chestnut hide, but it was time to walk first, stretch and ease tendons drawn tight by traveling nailed inside a box. Stretch him too, shake his mind open, let him feel the lifeblood going through the colt and remember just why he was here, what he'd been paid for. What little good he could do.

Willie was shaking his head as he walked slowly along the edge of the track, not keeping up, just walking. Blue felt the colt's edge, even with no bit he used the tied lead to tell the colt no; Curly shook his head but listened, kept to a walk, jigging sometimes but not breaking into the gallop he kept demanding. Blue patted the damp neck, felt the need in his own body but a run now wasn't good, they both needed time to settle, learn the land, hear the noises of motorcars and too many people – ah hell, Blue thought, and let the colt ease into a lope. Just a lope, no speed, give them both a chance to stretch and move out.

Goddamn; the colt was sound, strong, ready. No weakness, no fear, just a need to run. He leaned forward and whispered into the colt's flickering ears and the power came, drove them both forward in increasing and impossible speed.

It was downright beautiful and Willie Simms was smiling again. Whatever pricked at Mr. Mitchell, a good horse took off the edges, soothed the spirit. Now Willie knew he and the range cowboy were kin. It was how he suffered through the insults and meanness surrounding him; he rode a good horse, rode it well, won races because only he held that fragile will in his hands, felt the want, the go, the right time. Now.

He stopped walking, saw the rider's back, the long legs drawn up against the chestnut sides, the give at the shoulder, the body bent forward, still in a canter but the ache was there and Willie wanted them to run.

He knew too that sour-face George Bowdry was watching, so he thought hard, tried to tell his thoughts to Mr. Mitchell, that Bowdry wanted him to let the colt run, maybe even injure the animal, so Bowdry could be right, and Mr. Belmont he would listen to Bowdry and sell the colt and fire Blue. Send him home. Damn the man.

He'd not misjudged the cowboy; one slight forward lean and the colt bolted. Ran only a short distance before Willie saw the rider draw upright, ease the colt into a long trot, which the man sat well, some bounce but the trot slowed to a walk, the horse's head released, long and low strides sweeping them forward. Loose and relaxed, just what the colt needed and exactly what would make ole George mighty angry. Willie grinned to himself, was still grinning when Mitchell and the colt finished their one circle of the track, coming to a stop just at the closed gate where Willie patiently waited for them.

THIRTEEN

There were clothes in his possible bag and he smelled from the horse, the light gallop, so tonight in the dark he'd hose down, scrub himself clean with sand, sure was enough of it to scour his hide. Scour out old dreams and memories too; he was nothing to the child and meant to be nothing. He had to stay nothing, with nothing to give. Boy had him a pa and a beautiful woman who loved him and Blue didn't fit, wasn't meant to be any boy's pa, too much like his own pa, too hot in temper, too unforgiving.

It made him wonder what design that created humans and put this need in each of them, man and woman, saint and idiot and murderer, to lie with another and between them birth a child.

Most cowboys paid a woman for the need, and walked away, certain that the professional knew how to remove an unwanted seed trying to grow.

Men like Blue, unfit for human company, had no business breeding. They needed to be culled like the lamed or runt mustang stallions. Those got shot by ranchers wanting only the good quality stock to breed and reproduce themselves, the offspring caught and forced to become a working cow horse.

Blue's few memories of his own pa made him shake his head; there was a man needed shooting to protect his kin, his wife and child.

Hell of a thing to shoot a man for his chosen life, or to take away from him a need and force born in him. But it wasn't right, not in looking into that little boy's eyes, it wasn't right to hand down Blue's flaws of character to a child had no way to understand them.

That one moment with her still helped Blue; he used the memory to ease his constant anger. She had loved him one time, one night when she hadn't wanted to leave his bed. He'd made the decision for them by his running. It was what he did best, run from whatever felt too good, meant too much.

'Damn', George Bowdry thought. Another time then. It was obvious that Mitchell lacked the discipline to be bound by rules. And Bowdry would give him enough rules to bury him. It would be easy, done of course in Franklin's name. Bowdry was well aware of his own limitations but he had promised a nagging, temperamental wife that he would seek the head trainer's position, or indirectly manage a rise in some power and finances. He could tie his fortunes to the downfall of Blue Mitchell, making his own weakness less apparent to August Belmont.

It was closing in on evening and Blue'd not eaten all day. He knew if he said something, Willie would have an answer. And Belmont said there was a café.

Still he wasn't fit for human company; a wash under the ice-cold pump handle, a change into what passed as clean clothing, and he said to hell with it in his mind, he had no dignity left for it had been ripped out of him along with his heart this afternoon. He took the pile of stinking clothes, borrowed a water bucket and a few fistfuls of sand and set to work as his own laundress, scrubbing and rinsing, getting chilled, soaked in his only clean shirt, finally had to shuck out of his boots 'cause they were soaked, stood there looking at his misshapen feet, toes busted, a long scar from a Spanish dagger when he rode too far south from Tucson. White feet, bony toes all bent, he was for certain an ugly thing.

She'd seen him, naked head to toe, tended to his needs, washed and wiped his weak flesh and he hated what she knew about him. The scrubbing this time got him and his clothes clean, but it did nothing for the hunger and he couldn't find Willie the one time he walked the different shedrows, counted the empty and filled stalls. He wasn't going to call out or bother any of the other men; they didn't know him, couldn't trust him enough to even give him directions to the café.

He understood some of their fear, knew the effect of being the stranger, the different one, out of place. Hell, Blue figured, he was always out of place but his skin color wasn't what set him apart from other folk. If he could keep his mouth shut, his head down, he'd stay out of trouble. These men with their color had no such chance at all.

Damn shame, damn foolish.

Mr. August Belmont's name itself couldn't produce a meal for Blue right now. He'd been left penniless. And by god and by damn it all, Blue found he didn't much care. He'd been worse hungry before.

August Belmont saw his riders and grooms and walkers go into that disreputable tavern and café which they seemed to prefer, and it was easily discerned that they were a group unto themselves with no blond-haired outsider as uneasy company.

Belmont thought about it; he weighed and considered what he would do with Mitchell, where he might take the man that would not be uncomfortable, for either him or the eating establishment. That Mitchell himself might be uncertain in new surroundings crossed Belmont's thinking but he dismissed the concept as one belonging to an ordinary man, and Mitchell was far from that ordinary type of country folk who could not fathom city manners.

He found the man talking to the chestnut colt, which when he thought on it was perfectly reasonable, and why he had expected to find the man there by using reason and common sense.

Mitchell was somehow hunched down, looked like he was sitting on his boot heels, leaning forward from the stall door. The colt had his head and neck arched over the bottom half of the door, pulling at Mitchell's fingers that were raised over his head. It was a peculiar thing to watch, and Belmont hesitated, studied the man and the colt's response to him. There was trust between these two, and he wished to know how it could happen, that animal and human, without words or even compatible gestures, could enter into each other's world so completely. This shared understanding was a part of his acquaintance with horses that was missing.

"Mr. Mitchell!" The man turned his head slowly, grinned, nodded, then stood up to his full height, reminding Belmont that he himself was not a prepossessing figure. There was a grace and ease in Mitchell's move that most men of Belmont's acquaintance did not own. Their overstuffed bodies did not easily lend themselves to graceful movement, much to the dismay of their wives on the dancing floor.

In Mitchell's case, as in many of the cowboys Belmont had on occasion met, the ease of movement, the control of bodily motion, came as natural as waking up and needing to eat.

Mitchell answered Belmont's salutation; "Mr. Belmont." There was no 'sir', no half-bow or acknowledgment, simply a returned greeting. These western men did not allow another man any degree of social superiority.

"Mr. Mitchell, I am certain by now you are quite hungry, and I saw Willie and the others go into their café. It came to me, would you join me for supper? There is a place not too far from here, as I am sure walking is not your favored activity."

Mitchell studied his host, and a slow grin opened his face. "Mr. Belmont, you sure you want to be seen with the likes of me?" There was a hint of pride and derision in Mitchell's question, and what had started as pure charity took on the delight of challenging other men's perceptions as his own had been challenge by the purchase of a western Thoroughbred, and learning to accept the well-heralded genius of the man who brought the horse East.

Mitchell stood quiet while he studied August, and the knowing look in those wary, brilliant eyes was disturbing. Then he spoke; "Blue, I answer best to Blue. That's who I am, Mr. Belmont, no one and nothing but Blue."

All right, that was said clearly enough and August would respect the man's wishes. "Blue, there's a sporting club not far from here. The clients are racing men, owners, trainers and their ilk. I believe you would find the atmosphere interesting and the inhabitants quite colorful." Yourself included he thought, and saw the same thought go through the range man's face. This man was never to be underestimated.

"There is one problem, which with your approval, we can remedy quite quickly and it would be to your advantage to follow my lead in this matter." Blue nodded, that unruly blond hair covering his eyes for only a moment. Then he shoved his wide-brimmed hat on his head, sweeping the hair back so it did not interfere with his sight.

"You show me what you want done, Mr. Belmont." The man indeed did have some sense of manners.

He got shoved inside a men's clothing store, an unnecessary addition to his education. Belmont told him and Blue knew enough from a few places in Denver and Deadwood that a gentlemen wore a coat and tie at the evening meal at least and usually over a decently cleaned and ironed shirt.

The ragged shirt and hard wool pants with leather sewn to them, half-rotted boots, they weren't part of the acceptable dress for a gentleman to dine with companions. To Blue, clothing kept him covered and decent and nothing more, much like a knife was used for cutting. Dining in the evening with friends was like speaking foreign to him; food and clothing were nothing more than the necessities to keep working and not freeze or burn.

Stepping inside the shop hit Blue; it was filled with well-dressed men who bowed to Belmont while looking sideways at Blue. Then one particular well-dressed stout man with a good face, decent eyes, but too damned eager nodded and called Belmont by his name followed by 'sir', asking what he could do for the gentleman tonight.

Belmont's orders were quick; "He needs a coat, clean shirt, a tie and a new pair of boots. I wouldn't try the pants, he'll fight me there." Belmont knew Blue too well already; he nodded to the man, kept his own mouth shut.

The man extended his hand; "Albert Marquardt at your service, sir." Blue knew his manners, took the man's hand, was light on the grip, seeing as the face was white, the hands soft. "Blue Mitchell."

He did not expect the reaction; the hand was quickly removed, the face turned pale gray, the eyes flickering away from Blue, looking almost any place except at his new customer.

"I. . .ah, yes, Walter will take care of. . ." Belmont would not have it; "No, Mr. Marquardt, only you can turn our range friend here into an acceptable addition to any sporting club. I will pay extra of course, since I realize it is near to closing time."

"That's not why. . .Mr. Belmont, I have heard of this man." There his voice stopped, a slight cough, a hand held to his mouth. Blue stared; he'd never seen this man before, never heard his name or knew anything about him. And he'd done nothing yet in Brighton Beach to deserve any reputation at all. Hadn't been kicked out of a bar or hotel yet. He'd been no place this man would have seen him.

It grew hard to breathe and he knew Belmont was walking around the shop, talking fast, asking questions and telling the man what he needed to do, but Blue didn't care. He was numb, caught; he understood the meaning behind Marquardt's immediate distress.

Albert Marquardt had to be her husband.

Damn the coat was tight on his shoulder even as it hung on his gut, the shirt itched, it had one of those hard collars that Blue wanted to refuse and he could see in Belmont's face the man understood.

If he wasn't off balance and scared, Blue would have walked out, to hell with it, but he wanted to know about Marquardt, wanted to learn something about the man that he could hate.

Marquardt seemed decent, his touch quiet, never making Blue feel less than a man despite Belmont fronting the cash. It was the boots that did him in, half boots like Norris wore sometimes, no riding heel, no long shaft to protect his legs from cactus and juniper and anything else coming at a rider on a fast horse.

They were too easy to slide into, soft leather that would probably last just about the time of the home trip. But in the meanwhile, Blue figured he could walk some in these boots and not curse them. Then the man brought out several pairs of socks, soft knitted wool, nothing scratchy or hand-made. They made wearing the boots even more of a treat.

He couldn't find any reason to dislike Albert Marquardt.

The sporting club was a dark, thick-carpeted room, glossy floors gleaming around the edges, cold fire places with gold-colored grates in them, tables set around with thick chairs. Every head came up, several men half-rose as Belmont passed. He would wave a hand, or nod, but kept a straight line and Blue figured he best follow.

No one in the room looked at Blue; they wanted only Belmont's expensive attention. Blue was a nobody and after they got to the far wall of the high open room, he was damned glad none of these men wanted to touch his life or take a part of him. Belmont didn't have a moment's peace. Stopping, talking, listening, agreeing or disagreeing at his will, it took them five minutes to cross a few damned feet.

A white-coated man pulled out Belmont's chair and the man sat, waited while the servant pushed the chair in. That wasn't right to Blue so he hauled out his own chair and slid a leg over as if he was backing a rank horse.

The white-coated man stepped back, almost put a hand to his mouth; Blue grinned up at him and said, "Thanks, mister. Figured I could climb in on my own." The man turned and walked away, back stiff. It was all Blue could do not to laugh.

Then Belmont started on him; "Mr. Mitchell." He caught himself; "Blue, what went on between you and Mr. Marquardt? I have known the man for several years and he is nothing but polite, kind, and excellent in his chosen profession." Then the killer came; "I have met his wife, she is of the finest sort and is highly respected. She would not marry a deceitful man, yet you treated Marquardt as if he had committed a terrible sin."

Belmont hesitated; "He in turn, and this surprises me, treated you in exactly the same manner."

Blue had no answer; nothing could be said in his own defense since no decent man would ever betray a woman. The hurt of his thoughts closed his throat. He choked, and shook his head. Belmont ordered water, quickly, and a small young man brought a shiny glass, a large silver pitcher, and even poured out water before Blue could grab the pitcher and take care of himself.

Still he drank, wished it was whiskey, glad it wasn't, refilled his own glass before that helpful young man could catch the pitcher, grinned slightly as if the water helped and drank a half glass more before he tried speaking.

"Sir, Mr. Belmont." There it stood, no words, no possible explanation to a man he hardly knew. So Blue lied, or at least didn't tell the other half. "Guess I'm in a foul temper. I don't much like cities or lots of people. Went down to that beach of yours and took me a swim and I guess some of the folks watching didn't approve. Hell, all I took off was my boots and socks".

He realized what he was saying was a truth, just not the truth Belmont had requested. Belmont studied him closely; Blue held back his natural inclination to fight a man looked at him so, but he figured it was Belmont's right, bought and paid for with soft boots and the promise of a decent meal. It was a first for Blue, minding his manners 'cause someone put out a bunch of money on him. The feeling didn't set well.

Belmont pressed the issue; "That's understandable, however I am surprised you took out your temper on such an inoffensive gentleman. I gather you have not purchased clothes in such a manner before."

Here Blue had to laugh; "Mr. Belmont, my buying clothes means going to a dry goods store, finding these wool pants long enough, usually I got to sew on the leather patches, best thing for a man rides a lot of rough stock. And shirts, well they come in three sizes and the sleeves ain't usually long enough. That's it. No, I ain't never been measured and smoothed and tugged at before, not by a man. It like to make me damned. . .durned uncomfortable."

That seemed to ease the man's curiosity, for he wiped his mouth with the biggest and whitest napkin Blue'd ever seen, make a good-size sheet for most beds in a decent bunkhouse. 'We will order now' was all Belmont said and two gentlemen in black fancy suits stood to his attention.

Whiskey first, then wine with the meal, scallops and oysters and words Blue'd never heard until finally Belmont stopped, looked at Blue. "This is rude of me, sir, what are your preferences for dinner?" Here it was, the line between places and men; to Blue, dinner was the noon meal, enough food to keep a man going until the dark made work impossible. It was not a lengthy drawn-out waste of time with too much food and drink enough to make a man's head spin and give him nightmares.

"Steak, if you got a decent one, and something green 'though I ain't much on that lettuce. Whiskey'll do, no wine thanks. It gives me a bad head."

FOURTEEN

He passed by the sporting club every night; on a few occasions Mr. Belmont had invited him inside as his guest, but the line was drawn carefully, and only rarely were these invitations extended to the likes of George Bowdry.

Bowdry made the mistake of looking at the smoked glass; if he could see in, then his sad face could be seen by those enjoying the company and its surround.

He was there, that terrible rangeland cowboy who rode wild horses and spoke his piece and didn't mind or even notice what other people, important people, thought or cared.

That man was taking a drink of whiskey now, not sipping as a gentleman would do but gulps, almost loud enough for

Bowdry to hear. Head back, eyes half shut; those damnable eyes, blue even through the darkness of the bared window.

He put the glass down and said something to Mr. Belmont that had the man laughing, pounding the table with a soft fist, a gesture most uncharacteristic of Belmont's accustomed reserve. The gentleman was not given to expressions of emotion, whether delight, joy, or sorrow.

He knew the source of Mr. Belmont's reluctance around his second trainer. A few months ago, it had been given to Bowdry to explain the certain circumstances whereby Mr. Belmont's favorite filly, homebred and lively, had played too hard when turned out with her peers, intending to beat all of them in an impromptu race. She had beaten them only because she refused to slow up as the fence approached; she slammed herself into the fence and broken her neck.

The trainer at the time, Horace Danforth, gave that terrible responsibility to George Bowdry, who had at first refused, then saw the sign of dismissal in Danforth's expression and accepted the burden.

He had found Mr. Belmont about to enter the sporting club, and perhaps his choice of place and time had been remiss, but it was often difficult to keep track of Mr. Belmont's whereabouts, so he took the opportunity presented to him.

It went as he expected, with Mr. Belmont's anger placed on George's back; informing him that negligence had destroyed the filly, that she had been special and he would neither forgive nor forget her death.

Bowdry held his tongue as usual, and when, two months later, Mr. Danforth had to find more suitable employment with another gentleman of less money and poor manners, Bowdry actually expected to attain his goal of head trainer. And naturally that rise in stature and pay was denied him; Mr. Belmont saw fit to bring in an outsider. However he did grant George an interview, at Mrs. Bowdry's vehement insistence and appeared to have the decency to listen to George's plans and strategies for the horses.

There was some mollification in Mr. Belmont's praise of his organizational skills, his ability to find and maintain the highest standards in feed and bedding, and his control of the boys who worked directly with the horses themselves.

However, this small, pot-bellied, grandiose man with all the money and none of the foresight needed to run a fine racing stable on his own merits, denied George Bowdry his one last chance at greatness. At home, in the night, George lay next to his unforgiving wife and placed all the blame on one August Belmont Jr.'s blindness as to his trainer's worth.

Now there was Mr. Mitchell to enclose in that blame. Perhaps a vivid description of the man would give George's wife another target for her vile antagonism.

He turned from the exposing glass window and continued on his quest, to find a drinking establishment where he was not well known, where he could have a glass or two without such indulgence being returned to him in the form of gossip and Belmont's continuing disapproval.

"Mr. Mitchell, ah. . .Blue." Both men nodded in agreement that such a name was more proper than the foolish formality. Blue, however, knew not to cross the line and call his benefactor August, or Gus, or any such name. He might be lacking in education and manner, but he knew well enough where the line remained solid.

"We had made an arrangement for you to eat with Mr. Simms and the rest of the stable hands. What happened?" Now there was a fair question. Blue finished the last bite of his steak, best damned steak he'd had though he sure wouldn't go telling an Easterner that fact.

"I went swimming. Told you that. Didn't know how that salt when it dries will itch a man. Them boys at your barn were gone by the time I got back since I got myself lost." Here Mitchell's face changed, tightened only a moment but Belmont was learning the man's language enough to know a strong emotion went with that slight and unreadable gesture.

"I figured with the boys gone to eat, I could wash from that damned hand pump sets out by the stalls. I ain't too dumb to know that the shower you put in for the stable hands wasn't mine to use; that would be as welcome to them as some ranny using my saddle. Too personal, moving over their privacy."

Belmont leaned back in his chair; this man was endlessly fascinating. "So you showered, or rather bathed, under the hand pump?" He could not keep the surprise out of his voice.

"No, I ain't society-mannered but I know that much. So I pumped water and took buckets into the stall next to Curly. Damn that water was cold." The man nodded to the steward's offer of another pour of whiskey.

"How do you like this scotch, Blue?" Always that hesitation, he couldn't help it. Such a peculiar first name until one looked into those eyes.

"Well there, Mr. Belmont." No hesitation, only a sly grin. "Tastes some like the dirt I've dug through trying to find water. But it'll do unless there's a good bottle of rye handy."

Belmont had noticed that despite his rough nature and the stares his appearance garnered within the sporting club, Mitchell was quite well housebroken as he put it. Acceptable table manners, no reaching or grabbing, he even knew how to use a fork, while some of the westerners Belmont had dealings with disdained a fork as being a woman's tool.

"Where were you born, Blue?" The answer surprised and amused him; such names. "Musselshell, Wyoming, hardly there now. Ain't been back in twenty-some years. I'm guessing you was born in a city, went to good schools and know a whole lot about history and such. I like to read a book now and then, prefer histories if I can find them. Been reading. . ." Here his easy talk quit and it was that tight expression. A slow moment, then; "I worked mostly in New Mexico, some in Colorado and now with Con in Nebraska. This's the longest time I've stayed in one place. Con's a rare man."

Belmont studied the horseman, and found those eyes studying him in return. Blue kept going; "A colonel up to Fort

Robinson, south of Con's place, he told me horse-breaking was for young men. Well from what I see, horses won't make a man a decent living much longer. Racing, yeah, you'll pay the boys their small wages and they'll come and go, but them automobiles and trains, horses can't stand up to 'em."

Belmont laughed, took in a good swallow of fine scotch, coughed and shook his head. "How did you get to be so smart, Mr. Mitchell, without going to school?" The man had an answer, of course. "It ain't hard if you bother. I read, listen, pick up a paper when I can. That's how I knew your name, knew that Con wasn't getting in over his head when your trainer wanted to buy Curly."

"You look out for Con." "He's a good 'un, he's worked hard for what he has, and took me in when I was busted some." Belmont could imagine; the scars showed on the hands and face, what lay under the veneer of freshly purchased clothing would be more evidence of this man's existence. And from what little he knew, Belmont observed he would not wish to have shared most of those adventures.

They rose after another half hour; Mitchell's restless nature was obviously having difficulty with the concept of coffee and cigars and more visitors to their table, more questions, too much civilization.

Mitchell did have the manners to thank August for the supper, and offered to return the jacket since he'd have no more use for it. August smiled and nodded and said, no, you keep it, and noted silently that the man made no mention of returning the boots.

They separated, August headed to his office, Blue meaning to return to the stables.

Soft air brought that salt taste on an easy wind – he was too full, ate too much, drank too much. Damn, the rich life left him miserable. He shrugged out of the jacket, pulled off the tie, held them out at arm's length to study just exactly why wearing them made a man a gentleman.

"Hell with it." He rolled them up, stuffed them under his arm and started the walk back to the stables. This time he knew the direction.

An old man stumbled in front of him. Drunk but sober enough to mutter a 'scuse me mister' and make it up and over the walk, headed toward an alley. Blue stopped in front of the old man, gave him the wadded coat, letting the tie drop. The old man bent down, dark hands scratching for the length of material. 'Hold up my pants by god' was his reasoning and Blue nodded to the man's good sense.

They were seated in the drawing room, Albert with his evening paper, Dorothy with an unfinished bit of needlepoint spread across her lap. It was difficult to pick up the needle and thread it with the spun wool; her fingers were thickened, numb from her earlier shock.

She had to tell him, she'd tried a number of times, hinting at something not quite true in her story of widowhood, but her Albert simply waved away her concerns, saying with endearing truthfulness that if she were unmarried legally, preferably widowed but he would accept divorce, he did not need particulars. Illegitimacy was never a consideration.

It had been her son's reaction to the strange man that prompted her determination. All that afternoon he had spoken of the man, asking questions, wondering, tugging on her sleeve and wanting to know how she could know him. Who was he?

Robert was in bed now, the girls were sleeping, the house was quiet, its windows opened for evening breezes, one of the delights of living this far from the core of the City. During the winter, Albert traveled into New York, where his seasonal store generated good custom from those who had come to depend upon his sartorial services at the ocean. The summers kept them together, and pleased both Dorothy and her small son. The girls, well they had their nanny and were kept entertained, while Robert, ah yes Robert, held a special place she could not deny.

When word had come to her from the Fort that her oldest son had died, killed in a horse race, she had not spoken of her pain to Albert. She had not ever mentioned Joshua, for that would mean speaking of Harlan, and then explaining her first husband. A woman with such a past could not be truthful for society frowned upon these sordid events, never accepting that she had been the victim, not the instigator, in each tragic situation. Her grief had been necessarily silent.

Now she focused on the girls, played with them, gave the nanny a day to herself while she immersed herself in their innocence and delight. Still she had to struggle with the deep source of her distress; that it wasn't only Blue's shocking reappearance in her life, but that he had been there at the time of Joshua's death. The new commander had included that small fact in his report.

"Albert." His head came up from reading the paper. "Yes dear?" She took a deep breath; "I met a man today. Robert was fascinated by him." "I hope he was a decent sort and not one of the robber barons who so frequent our city. Or the riffraff so frequently seen at the race track." Albert could be pompous and decidedly middle class at times.

"Albert." His head jerked back. Dorothy took a gulp of air; "The man is Robert's father, no, you are his father but this is the man who. . ." She couldn't use the terms; sired was what came to mind, from discussions with Harlan Snow but that subject too was irritatingly indelicate for her to discuss, even with her beloved husband..

"He is the man who fathered Robert. And it is amazing how much our son looks like him." She hesitated, wanting Albert to take over but he had nothing to say.

And in truth when she could finally look at her husband, she had never seen his face contorted in this particular configuration. Pale, a tremble at the mouth, a refusal to look up.

He surprised her; after six years of marriage, her Albert surprised her. "Is he tall, has blond hair that needs cutting, a western sort who is here at Mr. Belmont's request? He has the most peculiar eyes. You spoke the name several times and while I didn't pay much attention, he would be notable if one were to encounter him." It connected then, she could see the knowledge go through Albert's mind, exhibited in the confusion on his face.

Each word he spoke hurt; "How could you, where. . .? I can see Robert's eyes in that man's face."

He shook as he held the evening paper, recalling that terrible man in his store, with Mr. Belmont giving orders. Mitchell had watched with amusement, he'd been sure that smile held an evil intent, as Albert tried his best to accommodate both Belmont's wishes and the cowboy's erratic temper.

He knew; his son's face was in those eyes, the hair, the shape and design of body and face, even down to the hands. This could not be true. Dorothy had sworn her husband had been a soldier, a military man killed by Indians. It could not be this hooligan, even though he was sponsored by August Belmont. Yet the uncanny match of form and face, boy to man, had immediately raced his heart and shortened his breath.

He had known then, despite the fact that his wife was only now telling the terrible truth. It had been August Belmont Jr.'s presence that kept Albert from demanding the lout be forcibly removed.

This nightmare entity, with the frightening stare, the free-swinging hair and lean body, could not be the man who captivated his Dorothy for even one night. It had to have been by coercion. He hoped that Mr. Belmont had either not noticed or had not been offended by Albert's tremors but he could not contain himself. The eyes on the westerner told him everything. Now his wife was corroborating Albert's suspicions.

He looked up, eager for such a terrible thought to be the truth. "No, Albert, it was nothing so savage. Can I tell you without further judgment? I love you, I have shown you that love for our married years. Please let that devotion guide you now in understanding." Albert Marquardt studied his beloved wife, saw her fear, knew it rivaled his and she was trying to tell a truth. He must be civilized and listen; he must trust love and accept what she had to say.

Her first try was so soft, the words stuttered into each other, that she stopped, took that breath again, and put together her courage and her terrible story. "I have lied to you. I had a husband who did not love me. And once, for one night, I was with a man who did love me." Her voice betrayed her again, she coughed and Albert made no effort to get her a glass of water. Oh, she thought. I have lost him.

"That our son, yours and mine, was born through love makes him special, Albert. He loves you as his father, he knows only you as his parent."

Simple, and devastating. Albert had a moment of desiring revenge, of hating the beautiful face as it told him an awful truth. Then he saw the tears and went to his wife, knelt beside her and took her face, kissed its sweet mouth and spoke the truth as it came to him. "I love you, Dorothy. And I believe you love me."

He needed to hear his own words out loud even as he pondered how he could punish or remove this man from their life. He could not bear her considering another man. It would become impossible for him to love her physically, knowing that one man, one time, had conceived and delivered both love and a child within her precious body.

Drinking shortened Blue's temper. Damn if that cur dog cut his path right now he'd kick it all the way to Kansas.

The shedrow was quiet, one light flickered in the building past the end stall, where Willie Simms and the track workers played cards and laughed and did not expect or want a stranger from Nebraska to interrupt their world.

Blue liked Willie, but he didn't know the others, didn't blame them for their reluctance. It was always the same in any bunkhouse, any spread. No matter the color of the newcomer, he was an unknown. And when a man dealt with horses, he had to trust his riding partner.

Then his natural suspicions pushed past the liquor and too much food. A shape slid through the door to Curly's stall. There was no cause for no one to be bothering the colt this time of night. Blue skimmed along the wood siding, leaned in over the door and Curly lost him the advantage by whinnying. The man stood up, grinned at Blue, and he knew he'd been suckered.

They'd been told to hurt him bad. Not kill him but damned close. Brass knuckles were a good start, work over the face were the orders, break a few ribs, maybe smash the hands. A policeman's billy club did great on the long fingers; damned man had been hit before, fingers bent and crooked, scars on the back. A good kick to the ribs, the son of a bitch rolled over and almost got up, no one got up after Tully kicked him that hard.

Man hung there, on all fours, coughed and groaned, blood ran from his mouth and Tully figured they'd done enough so he stepped back, signaled to the mug sent along to help him. Quit now, see what the son of a bitch was made of. Easy enough to kick him back down if he had the balls to stand.

Instead the son grabbed Tully at the knees, head butted the left one and Tully went down hard, groaning, finding the son of a bitch climbed on him, lay across his chest and grabbed his hair, slammed his head on the ground. Stronger than he could be, ain't possible that broke fingers and a stomped hand could grab a man's head. He heard the man's private groans in rhythm with his own but it didn't stop the ringing in his ears or the blackness come to his eyes.

"Damn it;" Tully yelled. He couldn't think of the mug's name. "Get this bastard off me."

FIFTEEN

Strange face staring at him; skin and texture he didn't know. Almost familiar but dark. No, Blue decided; light but not light like a white man. Coffee laced with canned milk, that was it. The way he liked his coffee, with a sweetener in it, molasses, or sugar if it was handy. Not often, though, a drifter didn't get many of those treats along the trail.

The pain reminded him; her hand holding a cup, pouring in canned milk to lace his coffee, brandy too, and sugar. Tasted the best he'd had. Partly because she served it to him. Pain was the same, more of it, more places, but still pain.

Willie. His voice starting rough, finding its strength as he said the name. A soft voice answered; "Blue, guess you gonna live. We didn't believe it and some of the boys, they wanted to make book but I told 'em you too good a man for us to be betting on your dying." Guess it must be bad 'cause it took the man a long time to find his stride.

Then Blue ran his tongue around his mouth, tasted copper, felt a rough-edged tooth, considered the many possibilities and didn't try to sit up.

"Good, man. You been here before, we ain't gonna have to tell you what you don't understand. Here." A glass, a tin cup actually, he took in the scent, knew the taste; laudanum.

"Mr. Belmont he called in a doc who wanted you to the hospital but you fought all of us hard enough that the doctor he got worried and said to leave you here. The boys and me, we said we'd do the doctoring, no man fights like that to not go some place, hell he's earned the right to be where he is."

Then Willie's face opened in a grin and Blue tried to match him but it hurt; goddamn it hurt. Willie touched his shoulder. "No, you keep still. You got yourself quite a visitor."

The face receded, he heard the soft words 'yes, ma'am' and couldn't think, wouldn't let himself go back in time. No.

The first glimpse of him stopped her; she felt her heart lurch, put a hand to her mouth to quiet her gasp but he must have heard for his head turned the slightest and even that small movement had to hurt.

The nice young man brought her a chair, set it close to Blue's head, backed away and gestured with his hand. He was a Negro, and Dorothy suspected he might well be the famous jockey that Mr. Belmont spoke of so highly. Her Albert had actually put a wager on one of Belmont's horses, and had come home smiling. He had taken them all out for a day's celebration, even closing the store, which Albert almost never did.

She had to keep thinking about Albert, using him, his memory, to keep her emotions under control, to not let anyone, including Blue and those men gathered outside, none of these people could be privy to how she felt. As if she could make any sense out of confusion.

At this moment she steadied herself on the back of the chair, bent down very carefully and kissed just above Blue's left eye, one of the few places on him that did not seem to have been bruised or cut.

Then she sat, feeling the chair shake and knowing it was her inner fears setting off the wooden shivers. She again touched Blue, on the shoulder, and he groaned. "Ma'am. You ain't meant to be here, to see no man in this shape. They won't even let me see myself so it's got to be bad."

She wanted to chide him, making jokes while almost dead. How could one man, then she remembered, it had been two men, how could they do this to a fellow human being. Then she clucked, she knew better, she'd married into the Army. How female of her to respond in a foolish manner.

"There isn't much for me to do this time, Blue. I would say a doctor has done his finest in sewing you back together." Blue raised a hand to touch the long scar on his face, short ends of black thread made it feel like a hungry insect.

"Don't think his work'll make me any prettier." She wanted to cry then, to pound on him and lie down beside him, tell him by small whispers in his ear he was the most beautiful man she'd ever known.

Instead she took his hand and laid it along his side. The touch of those misshapen fingers went through flesh to bone, directly into her center, the place this man had discovered inside her.

The touch came with a lesson; while she loved Blue, was thankful for knowing him, she adored and was in love with her husband. And in a part of her mind reserved for Blue alone, was the admission that he had been the one to open her. Without him, she would never have accepted Albert.

"Thank you, Blue." It was only a thought, perhaps becoming a whisper but his mouth moved into that wonderful charming, bruised and swollen grin and she bent down, for the last time, to kiss his mouth; whisper against his lips, to make it real for both of them. 'Thank you.'

He woke carefully, not moving but wiggling inside, thinking of a finger, an arm, finding less pain, some comfort. He must have slept a good long time.

She'd been here, clear in his mind, taste still on his mouth but it was a day ago, maybe more.

No one was around him now, no voices only silence, then a distant whinny and he was grinning, not much ache in that, so he reached up, found the stitched place wasn't sore and took the gamble. When a man needed to piss, it didn't take much to get him out of bed. Damned if he'd use that bedpan again. Willie Simms and his friends were saints far as Blue Mitchell was concerned.

He got into pants, looked down the length of his legs to his bare feet and figured they were better left unshod than risk him leaning down, even sitting, to shoe them. He'd been here before, looking down his own legs while thinking 'bout pulling on a pair of boots.

He hadn't tried it then either and clearly remembered splinters and hot dirt and the cool shade of a ramada, soft winds off the desert grass.

Standing up, spreading his feet so he kept his balance, he found that pulling on a shirt took more effort than he remembered so he gave up with one arm inside, one loose, got a button caught across his chest and ventured outside.

It was sand again, no damned Colorado rocks, just smoothed sand, even the manure was picked up, the path raked. These Thoroughbreds led an easy life, with nothing to do but run, eat, sleep, and drop more manure.

He found the outhouse but didn't use it, leaned up against the back, figured he had no business inside with naked feet. More sand accepted his waste; he watched the dark stream, saw no blood and sighed. He'd live.

Out on the track he could hear the hoof beats, feel the ground shake; then a wild whinny, a man's yell. Some cursing. Oh hell, he thought, horses and trouble wherever he went. Then he laughed at taking on what didn't belong to him. Easiest thing for a man to do. As if he were the most important being responsible for everything.

Blue was holding his ribs to laugh, feeling the release, the foolishness of his thoughts, when a chestnut colt came up sideways to him, trailing a lead snapped to a bridle, a saddle hanging off his ribs, and followed of course by a very dirty rider and a furious George Bowdry.

Without thinking Blue grabbed the lead, quickly moved Curly's curious nose away from his own ribs, patted the chestnut neck and spoke to the colt, calming him. The hide was wet, foam thick under the saddlecloth, yet the colt wasn't breathing hard, so the sweat was from fear more than running, which Blue immediately put onto Bowdry.

"Mr. Mitchell, you get back to your bed. The doctor told you to rest. . ." Bowdry had him a rough manner Blue decided; he couldn't be half-decent even to a man rising from the dead. Blue held the colt's neck, letting his weight rest on the horse, who lightly pushed against Blue's belly. He was surprised it didn't much hurt but felt good, a scratch of soft whiskers, their touch meant to soothe. The horse had come to him; he pressed his face into the colt's warm hide, drawing in the salt, that sweetness. All the sensations made Blue open his eyes, to see where he didn't want to be.

Then Bowdry became an angry man waving his arms and giving orders, red in the face, wearing peculiar clothes, a tight shirt collar, a flat straw hat. A Negro boy, not a man yet and small in size, came at Blue, close enough Blue recognized the face as one of those who'd fed and cleaned him.

He wanted to say thank-you for what the stable hand had done; he knew his manners, but the horse was taken from him, Bowdry shut his mouth while he rearranged the saddle and threw the Negro onto the colt and the chestnut reared, came down, snorted and took off with George Bowdry yelling orders no one could understand.

Blue made it back to the stall, to the narrow and stinking damp cot, the one chair, his few belongings. He sat in the chair, waited ten minutes of longing to close his eyes, then got up and put his boots on, finally shrugged into a cleaner shirt, no horse slime on the tails. Tucked the shirt inside his britches and stood straight up when he wanted to lie down. He needed to find Belmont, get paid, and get headed home. This damned city was too much for a Nebraska cowboy

The police had picked up two scratched and bleeding men hours after the beating. They were well known to the police, and consequently the law's first choice when August Belmont called and told them in hard terms what had been done to a man he valued and how he would react if the police could not find and prosecute the ruffians.

The obvious boss of the two wouldn't give a name of who gave the order or why, but he kept asking who the man was got to him so bad. "Son of a bitch," he was reported as saying. "That hooligan fought back even after I put him down.

None of this pleased Belmont, he did not care if a thug well known to the police admired the fact that Blue, when kicked half to death, still managed to drag down his attackers and maim them. What Mr. Belmont wanted was justice, and the name of the man who paid these for-hire bullyboys.

That name they couldn't give up, wouldn't even try when the police gave them their own version of a reminder. Didn't know, they said, an envelope of cash, a name, a description they didn't believe till they found the guy. No more information could be beaten out of them.

The results of the police investigation were far from satisfactory but August accepted what little information they had gleaned from their tactics. At least those who had meted out the punishment would themselves be punished further.

"Mr. Belmont, there is a. . .gentleman." Belmont rubbed his eyes, then his mouth. "It's fine, Taylor, send the gentleman in."

He pulled a chair up closer to the desk, was pouring out a freshly opened bottle of excellent rye into a crystal glass when the gentleman appeared. It was Mitchell, of course it was. The hesitation from his assistant had told him all he needed to know.

He indicated the chair, watched the battered man lower himself carefully. Then he handed him the whiskey, nodding as he spoke; "It's rye, Mr. Mitchell, what you once told me you preferred."

Mitchell looked at the glass, then up into Belmont's eyes and it was then, perhaps for the first time, that the esteemed August Belmont looked into the heart of a true westerner, and saw his own inadequacies reflected in the blood-shot gaze. When Mitchell spoke, it was obvious that words hurt but he would not quit until he had his say.

"Belmont." That took too much and Blue halted, gripped the chair arms; leather he decided, good cowhide well tanned. His fingers, the ones not taped together where they was broke, the few free fingertips ran a line on the hide, meant to remind him where he needed to be. And it sure wasn't in a fancy office of a horse owner who expected others to do what he commanded.

The other hand felt the ridges, edges, caverns of the glass, saw light chased into other colors, smelled the whiskey, more to his liking as the man said. A gulp, held in the mouth, scouring the remainder of those small cuts along his teeth and the inside of his mouth. Burned like hell and was honey at the same time.

He swallowed and looked up at August Belmont.

"How did you get here?" Belmont's tone held surprise and something else. Blue took another swallow, grunted; "You paid Con to send me into this hell with that colt you wanted so bad."

Belmont pulled back, took in a breath, then before he spoke his immediate thoughts, he looked closely at Mitchell and there was that smile; damn it, the man was actually teasing him.

"Blue." "Yes, Mr. Belmont." The man had the audacity to raise his glass and half-nod. He knew exactly what he'd done, and what August was about to say.

"If this is hell, Mr. Mitchell, then you are its devil." Harsh words yet the reaction was not what he expected; "I've been told that before." A deep breath, that slow grin; "It ain't new and it ain't always the truth."

"Blue." He decided to try again. "How did you get here?" "I walked. I've figured out your street signs and I know where the ocean is. I asked some man where the esteemed Mr. Belmont held court and he looked at me strange but told me your office address."

The chair held him close, the comfort from its padded shape and the good whiskey telling him to sleep. He watched as if from far away as Belmont filled his glass again with the smoothest rye whiskey and Blue took a sip, then a big swallow. He didn't hurt now, and he wasn't so goddamn tired. He looked down at the soft half boots and they belong in this world of thick rugs and polished wood and leather chairs that were clouds, feather quilts, things that didn't exist in Blue's life.

He woke with a start. Belmont was now seated behind his desk. "You walked here, from the stables?" "Yes sir." It didn't seem the right time for a smart answer. "And may I ask why?" Belmont's tone was even, despite the force behind that simple question.

Here it was, a place where his thoughts and rough thinking needed words he didn't own, couldn't claim. "Mr. Belmont, sir." He could here Willie Simms talking; it was always 'Mr. Belmont he.' Blue shook his head.

"I need to talk to the two sons a. . ." Oh hell, he thought. "I need to ask them who set me up. It was deliberate, them two sons had no reason to want me dead and that makes the beating from orders, not from their kindly dispositions."

As he had done quite frequently, August studied this man who seemed to have stepped out of a dime novel. In truth it was the thinking process that fascinated him, the untutored mind picking through happenstance and coming directly to the ugly and inevitable center of the conflict.

"What are your thoughts on the matter, Blue? Who have you so distressed that they would bargain with two minor thugs to ruin you?"

Nicely said, Blue decided, going over the words to be sure he understood all of Belmont's question. "I think you mean who in this here town, Mr. Belmont. I could give you a list of folks I've riled, hell we'll be here far into the night and you ain't got enough whiskey in that fancied bar to keep me talking that long. But that's a list from the past, I ain't been here long enough to make more'n a few folks angry enough to spend money."

Belmont simply cocked his head. "The police had several less than polite talks with the men and got no satisfactory answers. Their defense is their true ignorance."

Mitchell interrupted him and it wasn't appreciated; "They got paid in cash and never had a name, only a description of me and what to do. Damn." Belmont nodded; the man continued to infuriate and intrigue him.

"What will you do?" "I know only two gents might have it in for me, one I don't think'd be so damned mean, the other, .well he's got the heart for someone else to do the hurting, not the courage or strength to do it himself. And he'd enjoy every minute of what hurt me with great satisfaction."

Mitchell was quiet then, even wrapped the unbroken hand around the crystal glass and again Belmont marveled at the man's durability – from the doctor's report of the beating, two weeks in a hospital and several months of recovery would be normal.

It had only been five days ago since Willie Simms had found Mitchell outside the colt's stall. Rolled up in a corner, where manure had been raked to be picked up in the morning. Face down in the pile, bleeding out through multiple cuts, coughing up blood and manure when they rolled him over and Willie knew to call his boss. Not Bowdry, not the new trainer due to begin in a week's time, but the big boss, August Belmont.

"Mr. Mitchell." Belmont's concern was such that a first name, and especially one of such obscure elegance, would not be sufficient for his further comments. "Mr. Mitchell you cannot confront these thugs, nor can you search for their purported boss. You simply do not have the strength."

Mitchell grinned, of course he did, and then took a slow, long drink out of the glass of whiskey, put the fine glass down where the light caught it, sparkled blues and reds and yellows.

"Mr. Belmont, I was beat near to death on a man's orders. I owe him the same." He leaned forward, tried to stand and his legs wouldn't hold him. The man grunted as if something raw dug into him, and eased back into the chair.

"Guess retribution gets to wait another day or two." August shook his head. "I will summon transportation for you." Before Mitchell could object, August called; "Taylor, have Wilson bring the automobile around to the front."

Wilson told him it was a Duryea, built in Pennsylvania, and it was as if the man spoke a different set of words. The whole time spent in that office made no sense; whiskey and the beating had to have muddied his mind. The back seat wasn't as comfortable as that leather chair, but it beat walking and the machine didn't make too much noise. Wilson held on for his life to a raised wheel set right in the middle of the front of the vehicle and stuck out his arms left or right to tell those watching him where he was going next.

All Blue cared about was that Wilson knew how to get to the racetrack. Then the damned thing came to a sticky, bouncing stop and Blue bit on his mouth, held back the curses wanting to break out on their own. None of it was Wilson's fault, this mechanical thing had its peculiar way of going.

"Mr. Mitchell, sir, it is with regret that I am not allowed to approach the track and its environs any closer than this. The machine upsets the horses, sir, and as you know well, their fears can cause bolting and disasters. Here, let me help you down."

Never had a man needed to help him out of a carriage before, then again it was him usually doing the lifting for he didn't ride in carriages much, would rather be on the horse than behind it and this thing didn't even have a horse to pull it.

Blue nodded and almost fell down; half-drunk, and miserable. "I thank you, Mr. Wilson." "Wilson, sir, and you are welcome."

Edgar Wilson sat in the Duryea and watched as the cowboy finally regained his balance and managed to walk toward the shedrow. He had been informed about this gentleman's appearance, and how pleased Mr. Belmont was with the racehorse brought by the long-legged and obviously quite battered man.

Holding to Mr. Mitchells' hand and elbow, Edgar had a brief sense of what ticked inside the man; a pure strength and determination rare in those with whom Edgar Wilson worked. He was truly impressed, and worried; Mr. Mitchell had not yet met up with the racing crowd which preferred to choose its own winners and losers on the track.

Something told Edgar this inevitable meeting would not be simple or polite. The first beating had only been a taste of what was to come until Mitchell listened and did what he was told

Wilson shrugged and went back to the difficulties of maneuvering the Duryea back and around to remove all engine noise from the racetrack and its nervous inhabitants.

SIXTEEN

Willie found Blue leaning up against the colt's stall. That chestnut head was pushed around the wood upright, touching Blue's face, then his hand, then pulling at his shirt sleeve. Willie watched the performance and wanted to laugh; this odd-eyed man had him a rare way with the horses.

He even said thanks when Willie took his arm. Willie took in a breath and turned away for the man smelled drunk; how'd he get money for whiskey, or the whiskey itself? He wasn't strong enough to go traveling, and the local bars crowded round the track, they was home to thugs and all sorts of ill-mannered louts and they would have beaten Blue into a near coma and taken whatever money he had found to buy their own whiskey.

Then Blue nodded, almost fell over Willie and got stuck on the man's raised arm. Fell back, taking Willie with him and Blue said it; "Damn, son, I'm drunk." Willie laughed, "You be well drunk, Blue. I didn't think you were one to imbibe."

Propped back up against the shedrow wall, Blue studied Willie's face. "What'd you say?" "Drink, I didn't think you was one that had a taste for the whiskey." Blue thought about that statement, figured the man was right and tried to 'apologize but the words got stuck.

"Where's that cot, Willie? Can't remember just where I left it but I know I need to sleep."

He woke late, had no idea of time, knew he smelled like a skunk, felt like a rodent and rolled himself up and off the cot, found his boots and his way to the outhouse.

Then he half-drowned himself under the hand pump, water to wash, drink, scrub away stink and a sore head. After five minutes he felt close enough to clean, looked up at a row of stable hands grinning at him. He bowed, careful not to go too low, knowing he'd not come back up. Damned head rang like a bell but he stood straight again and the sons clapped for him.

His first visit when he was better-healed was to the clothing store of Albert Marquardt. He entered, remembered being here with Belmont, conscious that the fancy half boots they sold him were soaked, stained, smelled like horses and dirt. The coat was gone, the new shirt left in the stall, exchanged for one Blue'd had managed to wash out. Guess he looked like a bum for the clerk came from behind a counter and put a hand out to touch Blue's elbow. "Sir, perhaps you are in the wrong. . ."

Blue evaded the touch as he held his temper; it wasn't this poor son's fault that Blue'd come in to upset his safe world. He stepped back to give the man room, put both hands out, turning the broke one up palm first to show he was no threat, had no bad intentions. "Mr. Marquardt, I need to speak with him."

The runt shook and quivered, his lower lip going fast as a windmill in a Kansas dustup. Blue tried to calm him; "Son, I come in here before, with Mr. Belmont." The clerk flinched at the name, believing it to be a pure lie. Finally the son hid himself behind the counter and squeaked out 'Help!'

Albert Marquardt appeared, holding a rather large pistol and so uncomfortable with its weight and intended purpose that Blue put both hands in the air and said, "Don't shoot. I give up."

He had to keep from laughing, the movement hurt still but the look to Marquardt's face was worth the pain.

"Oh. It's you." Everything Blue had come to talk about was in that final word.

There was a world hidden behind the doorway, a table and chairs, a small stove, where Marquardt offered him a cup of tea, which Blue had managed to avoid most of his life, having been asked maybe twice, but Marquardt was so eager that he gave in. It was weird-tasting, like burned grass, but after a while he grew used to it; milk and sugar helped.

There wasn't much need for questions about the assault; Marquardt spoke of his wife's visit and her concern, and while Blue studied the eyes, he saw only compassion; no fear, no anger. His regard for the clothing salesman improved. And he braved the question because he had to know; "How's the boy? Robert?"

At the nerve of asking such a question, Marquardt pushed himself away from the table, rubbed his hands together and studied Blue deliberately. Between them, on the table but to one side, lay the lethal pistol. Blue had a feeling the slightly rusted weapon wasn't even loaded.

How dare he! To come in looking like a ragamuffin, one of those dreadful men living in the alleys, he even smelled like a sewer as he proceeded to ask such a personal question. Albert studied this man who had taken his wife's fancy, and her body, for a brief time so many years ago. He did not understand a woman's fascination with these wild men, unshorn, beaten, rough and untamed.

Still, Mitchell's voice was low, his words a pleading and in them Albert found sanctuary. He had what this man desperately wanted and knew he could not have. There was an unsuspected nobility to Mitchell, which Albert could not deny.

"Mr. Marquardt, I ain't asking to see the boy, or to have any part of his life. But I know who he is, and I'm betting from what your wife told me and how you're staring at me now, that she's told you the truth. She must trust you loving her if she could tell you. The world can be almighty brutal on a woman has a child this way."

It was a long and complex statement; Albert sighed, got up and walked around, standing for only a brief directly behind Mr. Mitchell. The man held still, perhaps not trusting fully but willing to give Albert his moment.

He returned to his seat and settled back. "You have been badly beaten. Dorothy advised me she had gone to see you. I was naturally upset, for her of course. But now I think I understand."

Two men with no words, both curious and unsettled; it was Albert Marquardt who attempted generosity; "Robert is a good boy, lively, as I imagine you were when a child." Blue shook his head. Albert asked; "No?"

Blue thought about it, how much to say, how to explain. "My pa worked me." The voice stopped, the vivid eyes shifting from Albert's face. "He wasn't the kind of pa you are." The man held on to the edge of the table, fingers bent against their taping, almost close enough to feel the gun's metal barrel.

"I grew up hard and I don't want my son." Here the man hesitated again and Albert could guess as to the impact of saying that one word out loud to another man who would know. "I don't want him to know any of what I've done. He's yours." That had to hurt, for it was a terrible gift for a man to offer a stranger. Blue stuttered; "Mr. Marquardt, Albert, take care of the boy, he's more a part of her and your wife is a special woman."

Blue Mitchell turned his back and would have bolted if his body could be moved that fast. He was able to stand and then push through the doorway into the fancy storefront and terrified the store clerk all over again, but he moved slowly, limping and powerless, knowing he had given away the only valuable thing in his life.

The long walk, no more horseless carriages for him, gave him time. He hated it, nothing caught his eye now, the women looked silly under their pompoms and umbrellas, there, he'd learned a new word, the men in those flat hats, dressed, stiff, choked on a tight collar and their own chosen hell.

He was a fool, beat up, alone and grieving for a boy he hadn't wanted, couldn't have and already missed terribly. One glimpse and he knew he'd never forget.

Now he knew who'd sent down the hired bums – that whey-faced pot-bellied George Bowdry.

Good thing he was walking and tired, foot sore, ribs hurting, or when he finally got to the shedrow and the stalls and the training track, there would be bits and small bloody pieces of what had pretended to be a man spread all over the goddamn place.

Blue spoke the oath out loud, and again, until an old man in a filthy coat stopped and put his hands up; "Sir, I ain't done it, no it weren't me. You go 'long, mister. You take that talk someplace else."

Bowdry watched Mitchell walk down the shedrow to where his stall was. The man belonged in a stall, like the other horses' behinds that were part of the 'Belmont string.' Until the new trainer, a more sophisticated and acceptable gentleman, so he'd been told, came in to take over, George Bowdry was still in charge.

He was busy with the schedule, modifying what Franklin had told him, nothing enormous, but he wanted that chestnut colt run hard, and soon. Simms kept taking the colt out for easy gallops, even though the boy was close to retired. Had him a feel for the chestnut, Willie said. A flighty thing of little breeding although papered with the Jockey Club. George didn't like the knowing eye, the flash of speed with fading stamina behind it, and the colt didn't like him, tried to take a bite out of whatever part of George Bowdry could be reached whenever it came close enough.

Tomorrow, he had scheduled a speed trial. With several of the young colts and one filly, although he did not feel the fillies could keep up with their male counterparts. Mitchell wasn't healthy enough to bother or interfere, or to offer to ride. Mitchell riding was something Bowdry would like to see up close, rather than watching from a distant window; listening to Simms speak of the man's talent made him wonder if perhaps he had judged too harshly and far too soon. However such an exhibition would not further Bowdry's plan so he was satisfied that Mitchell's unfortunate beating had served its purpose.

If the colt was any good, then George would set up a special training schedule. There were numerous races for three-year-olds at Sheepshead in the late summer, including a futurity around Labor Day. If the colt had speed at any distance, there would be a race on the card for him.

But George intended to push the colt hard to prove his point that unless a racehorse had good bloodlines, it was most likely an also-ran.

"You looks tired." Blue had an easy answer; "Willie, more'n tired I need a good meal. You take me to that café?" Willie nodded, yes, that would be a privilege.

It was slow walking but Willie didn't mind. "I been riding that colt, you call him Curly, he's got a good mouth, and a long stride. So far that George Bowdry he been pushing me to run the colt but I been giving him sprints after an easy gallop. Give him time to get used to the air 'round here."

The idea made Blue laugh; "He comes from up on the plains, Willie. The land stands higher so I'm betting this air gives him extra run." Willie walked a few strides, head turned, face thoughtful. Then he stopped. "That explains why I felt that colt always asking to run. Didn't come to me 'cause he was all that time on the train and then out on your prairie and it never figured he'd be more fit rather than out of shape.

"Mr. Blue Mitchell, I'm buying you the best ribs in town, my treat. I can trust what I know, figured he had him an edge but didn't understand it. Tomorrow's gonna be a day of reckoning."

It was dark and rich inside the diner, faces turned to him but he was used to that. No different here, in the East, in a bar of Negroes eating and drinking. Hell he wondered where he'd ever find a place no one looked at him with war on their minds.

The food was good, and no one came to their table for a quarrel. They all nodded greetings to Willie, and the man nodded back, sat across from Blue, talked as if Blue were his best and closest friend and left the clients of the diner and bar to tend to their own lives.

It was more questions about horses and what was it like in Nebraska, he'd never been west of that big muddy river but he'd been to England and liked riding there 'though it was too wet for him, now he liked the beach, but he had trouble with some of the practices. This racecourse, when they had a good runner, why the boss he hired thugs, could even be those that beat on Blue, the boss hired watchmen to keep watching through the night 'fore a big race. Some of them bad folk'd take a horse out at night and run him till he was 'bout to drop and then they bet on the other horse to win, knowing what they knew. Cheating on good folks come out for fun, or the owners wanting a sporting chance.

Blue missed about half of Willie's words but he caught the thugs and the night-racing and it came to him he wanted out of this damned town soon as he could. He needed a few more days to see the colt run, and to settle with George Bowdry before he got back on that train going home.

It was early, almost sunrise, and Willie wore thin pants, high muddy boots, a hat turned backwards to evade the wind. Blue went to saddle the colt, who pushed against him, then looked out to the track as if he knew.

Curly was rubbed down and glossy, mane and tail trimmed; Blue stepped back and studied this colt he'd known all his young life, and finally saw a racehorse instead of a wild-eyed range bronc.

Throwing Willie up on the colt took some toll on his ribs but it was right, he and Willie knew. No one else needed to be fooling with the colt's mind or his gear. Willie settled light, the colt nodded his head and pushed one more time against Blue's arm and then accepted Willie's touch on the rein. Time to go to work.

Watching the colt listen to Willie, start square, run easily, move out when Willie's hands seem to loosen the rein, his body came closer to the colt's neck, and Curly responded, lengthening his strides, ears pinned, tugging at the rein, running as he needed to run. Blue was split; watching the pair race was beautiful, knowing he could no longer ride the colt hurt like a fresh wound.

Then a dog spilled out onto the track, yelping, tail down, running away from something unseen. The colt saw his attacker and remembered those damned Nebraska wolves; he went high in a leap sideways and then bucked, kicked at the skittering dog who kept yelping.

Willie's skill was admirable, when Blue had time to think on it later. The man was tossed forward, then slid to one side, went up with a downward buck, caught the reins, clamped his legs and rode out the worst, then asked the colt to run again and Curly left that part of the track as if a demon was chasing him.

The colt went wide around a turn, hit up too high off the track, Willie steered him to the middle, the colt fought, bucked again and Willie used a stick this time, tapping the colt on the right shoulder. Blue almost heard the scream of anger from a colt who'd never been hit. The long tail thrashed like a cat and the small head went side to side and Blue thought 'hell' but then the colt straightened out, the dog was gone from the track, and Willie stood up in the stirrups, eased the colt down to a lope, then a trot, then finally, to everyone's relief, a long, sweeping walk where both rider and horse could relax.

Bowdry was at the rail. "As I thought, Mr. Mitchell, that colt is nothing but a wild horse. It will take months to train it properly." Bowdry moved away quickly, before Blue's bunched fist could reach that puffy nose and maybe tap it one or two times.

Willie and the colt drifted over to where Blue stood. "That wasn't no accident, Blue. That dog he belong to Mr. Bowdry and he kicked his own dog, meant to hurt him. It were downright mean to scare a good colt like this. If he'd got loose. . ." Blue studied Willie's face, saw no fear, only a raw anger he could match with his own. He walked back to the shedrow with Willie and the colt, one hand gentle on the colt's neck, Willie's hand allowing a loose rein.

"You're one hell of a rider, Mr. Simms." He stopped the colt, stood at the bridle and looked direct into Willie's face. "I know you're a winning rider and all that, but you know your horses and I'm mighty pleased you're on Curly, he needs to trust the man telling him what to do."

Such things weren't said between white and Negro – it was a few extra dollars, a 'well done, boy' with maybe a pat on the shoulder. But to stop and look at him, those hard eyes clear, to say those words one horseman to another, was the best thing Willie had heard from the world outside his family.

An hour later Blue walked back out to the track, watched a few more of Mr. Belmont's fancy-breds get their morning gallop. And near George Bowdry, off any tie or leash but sticking close, was a scruffy dog with black spots and an irregular patch on its back. It looked a whole lot like the cur dog kicked out into the track meant to terrorize Curly.

The connection between Bowdry and the dog wasn't any surprise to Blue; he didn't get mad or lose his temper, no words reached his mouth without going through his brain. First time in his life maybe he thought ahead and figured he'd keep this bit of information, use it when it was needed.

He went and walked the colt that afternoon. Curly was plumb jittery at the track, head turning, ears swiveling, looking for that small black and white yapping bit of trouble. Blue'd thought so, it was his reason for taking the colt out. He knotted the lead to the halter, swung up, groaned some as his ribs and a few other places on his back had some strong things to say about beatings and too soon, but Curly didn't hump up or shy. The colt stood, then bought his head around and sniffed Blue's boot toe and eventually they went for a walk.

Bowdry came flying out of his office and the colt spooked, Blue slid with him, swallowed hard, then spoke his piece; "Damn you, mister. You don't know nothing 'bout horses. You keep scaring this colt and he'll never run."

There it was, flat out between them. "I do believe you are exaggerating, Mr. Mitchell, and I also believe that you have no permission to be riding one of Mr. Belmont's colts."

Blue lowered his head, touched Curly's withers with his taped fingers, raised his eyes back up, stared at Bowdry with all the fury he could find. The man backed up a step; good.

"You ask Mr. Belmont, Bowdry. You see what he has to say." He tipped his head, pushed the colt around with a knee and a tug on the inside tied lead and they sauntered down the outside of the track rail, where horses loped along, or were running side-by-side. Nothing to get excited about, that's what his hands, legs, and heart were telling the restless Nebraska colt.

He needed this, to be on a horse again. Despite the twinges in his ribs, the itch on his face where those damnable stitches stuck out like crusted dirt, he was whole on a horse, a man again, not no swamper or shoveler or sport for a rich man's fancy.

Curly tossed his head, it couldn't be against a tight rein so Blue let his legs touch Curly's ribs and the colt in one easy step moved into a lope so smooth a man could sit up there all day, have a cup of coffee, maybe even roll himself a smoke if that was to his liking.

It was all the colt wanted, what he needed, no one holding or pushing or kicking or stopping him, just a lazy stroll around the outside of the track, passing the working horses galloping in the opposite direction, giving the soul of both man and horse a moment's place to heal.

When he put the colt up, knowing it was time when he slid off and the colt nuzzled him, those dark eyes soft, no white showing, Willie was standing between the colt's stall and where Blue had been staying. His dark hand held a small white square, and while Blue noted it as something unusual, he didn't think on it while tending to the colt. He rubbed the light chestnut hide, smoothed down the sweat marks, felt each leg, carefully holding the tendons; cool, hard, firm. Nothing wrong with this colt's legs.

"Here. You take this. A boy he come give this to me after I says I know you. I ain't moved since he give it to me. Feels heavy, too nice for the likes of us. You and me." There had been that smallest hesitation, before the word linking them together was said out loud. But they were alike, men who came alive around horses, who were less than wanted when they were isolated from what they knew. Willie's hands were magic; Blue only hoped his bent fingers held that same touch. He'd pulled off the strapping yesterday and the fingers could be moved, they flexed some and didn't hurt much. He eyed Willie's slender fingers, saw the stark white paper and had an immediate reaction in his belly.

Willie dropped his head, held out the envelope. "Thought that might be it," he said. Then he shook his head; "She's a nice lady. She come here when you were down and sat with you, took care of you. How come a woman like her would tend to you I don't know, but that one, she's a real lady."

Blue felt the odd sensation of owing this man a small piece of himself. "Years back she and her. . ." He couldn't say it. "She tended to me when I got myself kicked pretty bad and needed some stitching. Got her a fine hand with a needle." It was only half a lie and close enough to the truth.

Willie laughed, leaned back some and looked straight into Blue's eyes. "I seen you, Blue Mitchell, I washed you like a baby and I counted. Hell, man, there ain't no reason for you to be with the rest of us live folk."

There was nothing to do but laugh. "It was that left arm, Willie, a mare gave me hell for helping her birth and man she laid into me. That lady, she splinted and tended to me for more'n a week."

Willie's response wasn't what Blue expected; "Don't take much time healing do you? What I seen, you should a spent most of your life in bed." Then, in an odd moment of sharing without reservation, Willie grinned; "Either the ladies or a bullet, you must a spent most of your life on your back, if you wasn't on a horse."

His face got hot, he felt it, made him sweat, but he couldn't get angry; Willie was laughing and by god he was right too. Blue lifted the white square envelope; "She is a lady, Willie, and whatever it says in here, I ain't good enough for her kindness."

He left it, couldn't bear the look on Willie's face, the knowing eyes, no smirk or grin, nothing wrong, more sympathy than anything crude. "Thanks, Willie." "For what, I done nothing but stand here and hold that white thing." Blue had to laugh again; "You know. Thanks."

SEVENTEEN

He found the address after wandering for a half hour. In a nice place of course, trees planted on the streets, houses set back, mansions to his eyes but he knew the difference, had seen the real palaces with acres of lawn and people out digging and cutting and doing all those hard-labor chores.

Here a man could be expected to trim the small grassy square in front of his home, the woman of the house could sweep the steps without losing any social standing. It was a nice building, where children were safe and doors didn't need to be locked. A house of brick and stone with carved doors and high windows, a roof made of what looked like sliced gray rock.

The white envelope was smudged and torn; in his haste he'd yanked it open, almost divided the address so he wouldn't know where to find her. That envelope was folded close in his shirt pocket. He was wearing the fancy shirt Mr. Belmont bought him, and he almost wished he had that coat went over it, not the tie though; he agreed with the old man who'd took the coat, ties were only good for choking a man or holding up his pants.

Since he didn't have a penny, and wouldn't ride in one of them trolleys or ever get in a motorcar again if he had the money, he was walking, glad for the half boots, kind of laughing at himself. He'd never walked this much, not in all the times a bronc threw him and he had to walk to wherever home was at the moment.

The stone steps were worn with folks' coming and going; he managed two of them and had to stop. She was inside and so was his son and he was terrified.

The door opened and a small boy appeared; they met about eye level as Blue stood down maybe five steps. Behind the boy were two smaller children, girls he figured out, hair in braids, pretty dress. Long shiny dark hair, like their mother. The boy's hair was almost white, even at a distance the eyes were vivid and Blue had the strangest sense of seeing himself as the world saw him. Eager, unreasonable, hot tempered.

The boy, Robert, came down the steps running, slammed straight into Blue knowing that he would be caught, safe, held in the arms of this cowboy who his mother said was a good friend from so many years ago. A real cowboy.

The hands were small, their backs lightly tanned, the palms pink and unscarred. Perfect hands that grabbed around Blue's broken fingers and he kept the unexpected groan to himself. Then her voice; "Robert, let our guest come inside, and be careful, he was injured not too long ago." She was smiling at him over the head of their son, a look in her eyes close to the panic inside him. They both knew a boy would have to ask.

"How'd you get hurt, Mr. Mitchell?" Blue glanced quickly at her, saw that the girls were holding to her dress." I work with horses, son." He dared using the word, it could mean a term of affection, it was what he called a bronc he was trying to ride, keeping his voice low and even to not scare the youngster.

That face, the eyes; "But cowboys don't get bucked off." Blue laughed, some things were always the same. "Boy, Robert, there ain't a horse can't be ridden, ain't a cowboy don't come off every so often. It don't mean he can't ride, it wasn't his day is all."

Robert looked at his momma; "He talks funny, Mama, not like you taught me."

There it was, said by the child himself. Blue leaned his weight on his right foot, readied to turn, when the voice of Albert Marquardt stopped him. "Come in, Mr. Mitchell. We thought we would eat in the garden. The children have helped their mother prepare the table outside. It is much cooler under the shade tree. Please come in, sir."

The man looked straight into Blue's eyes and smiled and it was obvious he meant the invitation. Then the boy ran up the steps and grabbed one of Marquardt's hands. "Papa, Papa, he's a real cowboy and everything."

He'd never go back, never sit at a table with small children while they asked endless questions, and then listen as mother and father, that hurt but he made himself think it, answered or asked a question in return that made the child think of his own answer.

It was nothing like what he'd known, and now he could be easy about the boy, knowing he was loved and cared for in a way Blue didn't know existed until that one meal outside under a tree, laughing, learning to enjoy and not fret about what might be expected of him.

And he'd come to respect a man who made a living building clothes for other men to wear, a job meant for women and girls, nothing to challenge a man, make him figure out danger and face it. The man came home to his wife and children and talk about small daily things and that same man was raising a smart, caring family. Blue's one exposure to such living left him angry, more lonesome, and determined he'd never sire another child. He could never be the father he saw in Albert Marquardt's every word and gesture.

He made his manners, said 'thank-you' too many times and yet when he escaped through the front door to those worn steps again, into a cool night with no talk or noise except the far-away outside world, the small boy grabbed him, took his hand and made him crouch down. The move hurt Blue's ribs and again he didn't care.

"If when I grow up and go out to where you are, will you teach me to be a cowboy?" He didn't need to see her reaction; he could feel it inside him as well. "You listen to your momma, boy, do as your poppa says. You learn as much as you can, then maybe you can visit. But the cowboy life's going away, boy, I know it, and hate it. But when I'm an old man there won't be no more cowboys."

The small eager face turned solemn and Robert Marquardt marched back into the house without turning one more time to say goodbye.

Albert Marquardt took his small brood into the dark of the house, leaving his wife and her one-time lover with a peculiar privacy. He was taking an enormous risk, but Albert had watched his wife during the meal, and Mr. Mitchell also, and by now he felt he could trust them both.

"Blue." He couldn't stand, legs giving out under him. He sat, thanking the step that caught him. She did something with her skirts and sat down next to him, not close, too many neighbors watching, so maintaining a proper distance between them was extremely important while doing something highly irregular. Sitting on the front steps and talking, a well-known wife speaking with a ragged stranger. But the words needed to be said.

"We never spoken about Joshua." He couldn't bear the name so he turned his head, thought of getting up and recognized his battered flesh would not hold him. She was insistent.

"Colonel Radcliffe wrote and told me of the terrible circumstances." The space between them wasn't wide enough, Blue wanted to shuffle and slide away. "He said that you went back for Joshua, that you were the one holding him when he died."

Blue leaned on a hand, pushed the edge of the palm up against his face, covering his nose and mouth. The lightest touch of two fingers on his upper arm, where it had been broken, shocked him.

"Your being there, at the end, knowing someone he knew was. . ." She couldn't finish, she was crying, he didn't need to look. Blue put his hands between his knees, looked at them, remembering them as they cradled the boy's head, the eyes watching him, fading, then shutting down. Gone. His voice was rough; "He told me where you were, that I had a son."

She nodded; he could hear the rustle of her clothing. "He knew Robert was his half-brother, he was the first to see at the time Robert was born. He championed me but Harlan. . ."

"Joshua was a friend, ma'am. I was responsible. . ." She tapped his shoulder. A tap meant to draw and keep his attention. "He does not belong to you that way, never, Blue. He was a man, and oh how he loved to race a good horse. All through school. . .you were there, you held him, he wasn't alone. Leave me that much before you go away. Joshua made his own choices. He was a young man with great sense."

It had been on his mind and now he spoke it without seeing how it would affect her, how it could be understood in a different way. His voice growled out the words; "Why do you call him Robert? He's a child, give him a child's name. It sounds like you're always scolding him or angry, when you say his name that way."

He felt her pull back, draw in and he wanted to look at her, to wipe out the tears, soften the pain of what he'd said. But in his life he remembered that the hard saying of his name always came before a whipping and even though he knew she and her husband did not hit the children, he could not help the connection in his mind. The boy was him, a second chance, and fears of his own past made him speak.

"Ma'am, when I work a colt, I speak soft, easy words, call it 'son' or 'girl' and it's quiet between us. When that same colt or filly doesn't listen or acts bad, I use a harsh name, whatever I've been calling them. Rocky or Star, Two Spot or something like that. They know, when I use that tone and their full name, they know they've done something wrong. There ain't no need to treat the boy such, he don't appear to be much trouble. Not like me at all."

Her words surprised him; "You don't remember, do you? I must have asked when you were so ill and you answered, telling me it was a secret you never shared. I was flattered that you trusted me that much, giving me a piece of you so raw with memory."

Only then did the meaning of his first question, the words after it, the different way of what he was saying begin to make sense. And yes, more than likely, he did not remember giving her his name, but his perspective was from that child's view, a child's pain, and it never occurred to Dorothy that her use of the formal name might create a different feeling than she had intended. She had only wanted to hold Blue's secret next to her, and calling the boy by his full adult name was her small way of keeping a piece of her son's father.

This time she turned completely toward Blue and nevermind those busybodies on the street watching through their lace-curtained windows; looking at his face, her eyes traveled those once-loved features, firming him in her memory.

She had forgotten this about him, how he could in his untutored and uneducated way dig out what was important. That he would take up for his son pleased her.

"I will call him Robby, for you. And I understand now what you said. As if I am chastising him each time I speak his name." Blue grinned at her and she fought back wanting to touch his battered face. "Ma'am, I'm guessing on that 'chastise' word means scolding. And I'd right appreciate it if you'd use Robby. The sound lies kinder in the mind."

It was getting uncomfortable setting next to the woman. He was remembering all sorts of things a decent man did not think of when he talked with a woman like Dorothy Marquardt. It was time for getting. "Ma'am, I'll try to let you know where I am, where I'm living at the time. Just so if something happens."

She remained seated as he struggled to get up; no, she could not help him. A window across the street had its curtain pulled back. She stared at the interloper and the curtain dropped. She did not want anyone to see his condition, the limp, the bruises that made him appear vulnerable. There was nothing soft or simple with this man.

She watched him, bit her lower lip hard enough that she tasted a tiny speck of blood. Good, she thought, I can feel some of his pain now. Talking to herself in such a manner was foolishness; the pain they shared had nothing in it of the physical.

He wouldn't touch her, didn't try to shake hands, not even the slightest brush of his fingers on her arm. No one was watching or if they were it was none of their business but he knew what was right. She didn't call him back or stand with him. He knew the way to the track shedrows; he walked slowly, trying to feel the movement within his body that would keep his mind from thinking.

He managed his way out of the nice neighborhood, down an alley, past a bar, then a long stretch of bars and taverns and men shouting, laughter, even a piano as he passed one open door. A man bumped into him and he stopped, wanted to fight but the man nodded a 'sorry' and kept going. Goddamn.

Three city toughs were leaned up against a wall, smoking cigars, laughing too loud and one voice hit a nerve that stopped Blue. He stared at the wide shoulders, the tilt of the thick head and knew with complete certainty; he went at the man hard, fists readied, wishing for a knife or a gun but goddamn this man was his attacker.

He found the jaw first, sent the man sideways, got to the gut, another blow and then a second, heard the grunt, smelled the stink of exploding breath and used his elbow against the ribs to shove one of the bullyboy's friends to get the hell out of the way, it was a private fight.

When the thug's hand went into a coat pocket, Blue grabbed through the cloth, felt the hard edges of those knuckles that'd cut his face. "You son of a bitch you damn well fight your own battle. One on one, rest of you boys stay out of it."

He stopped a moment, conscious of noise, then a false quiet. There were men, five, maybe ten, a few more coming out of other bars, watching, heads shaking. One man came forward holding a billy club and was grabbed by three bystanders.

"Tully earned this one, boys." A voice Blue didn't know but he nodded to where it came from and spoke his own piece; "Just him and me, boys, the damned rest of you can watch if you want. It ain't going to be pretty."

He ducked on that last word, already knowing Tully's methods. Sure enough a fist and arm went sliding past his head and he hit in close, two to the ribs, one more to the jaw. Tully kicked up hard; Blue twisted and the steel-toed boot cut into his shin. He grinned, ducked another blow that raked a cheekbone and took out some of the rotting stitches. He laughed and Tully stepped back swearing but hands pushed him into Blue and Blue nodded thanks as he knocked out two of the thug's teeth.

Tully spat blood, kicked at Blue again, who tried to spin, got caught on the hip and went to his knees. Crossed his arms to fend off the heavy boots, heard a crack, clenched the fist and knew it wasn't broken. Blue cried out as if the arm tortured him and Tully stopped, turned to the audience to have his moment and Blue slammed into him, took them both down, rolling and kicking, once again slamming Tully's head, feeling that thud, wanting the thick body beneath him to struggle until it was ended.

"No. You stop now." The voice slowed his hands, seared into his mind. Horses, racing; the boy Joshua; it was Willie Simms and his kindness that broke through Blue's anger.

The crowd growled. No other way to hear it, and Blue had a choice. He dropped Tully, stood up best he could and limped to Willie's side. His head cleared and he recognized what the jockey had done for him.

He said his piece, the men listened; Tully lay unconscious but Blue could see him still breathing. "If you gentlemen don't mind, me and my friend'll go back to the horses. Leastways they beat up on a man fair."

He couldn't let it show, not to anyone, not even to this small man who stood up to a crowd, especially a crowd of white faces and bad tempers that would easily kill him and then go back to their drinking. Inside he was shaking, trembling so his back teeth chattered. He stumbled and Willie tucked his shoulder under Blue's arm quickly, then as Blue steadied the man backed away.

He wanted to spit out the taste but his mouth was dry and the taste was anger, not blood or bile. Anger that pushed him to want a killing. There was blood, but it was from torn stitches and new cuts. He wiped at the mess, saw on the sleeve of the fancy shirt too much of his own blood, bright red clots and thin runny liquid and he hated himself, hated the need to strike back, to hurt as he'd been hurt.

His body began to respond to his will, legs moving with less pain, ribs able to let him breathe, eyes clearing free of rage and he began to taste the salt air again, the smells of the city. In the back of his memory was the time he'd spent with his son. The husband and those two girls lingered behind the boy's mother. The child, Robert, Robby, was unique, the only future proof that Blue Mitchell ever existed.

He shook his head, felt that hair slap his neck as a reminder of how often he'd fought, been wounded, what he fought for, mostly his right to stay who and what he was. He grinned, nothing else to do; he'd gotten away with it, with being alive one more time.

EIGHTEEN

Mitchell was too bloody for Willie's comfort. Still he had that look, maybe he stumbled a couple of times, needed a nudge from Willie to stay upright but then that grin reappeared and Mitchell was smart enough to stop once they got out of sight. Man was something Willie never come 'cross before; he just plain didn't give a damn.

"Willie, you saved me back there." Willie sighed but Mitchell wouldn't let it rest. "I mean it, I felt what I was doing and wanted doing it and I ain't the kind of man takes pleasure and need out of killing. I saw him and no man beats me like that. No man, but I ain't wanting to be a killer. So, Willie Simms, you just saved a man from himself."

He'd never thought on such a thing. Life at the track for Willie was guiding the colts and fillies and listening to the man tell him what needed to be done and Willie doing exactly what he thought needed doing and bearing the anger or accepting the praise, each time knowing it was his instinct did right and carried them home.

This man, he confounded Willie by talking about the soul instead of hoof beats and the feel of an eager horse wanting to run. It was a first time for Willie, that a white man talked to him without color.

From what he'd seen, this man had himself too big a share of trouble, so he knew the value of each life, each day; it made Willie angry to think of folks wanting the man's hide.

"Willie, you knew what doc to call last time, think I need another visit, maybe this time I can walk to his office. I don't want to always be flat out when he works on me. 'Sides, he said come to him when it was time to pull these damned stitches."

Willie looked at Mitchell's torn face. "Looks to be that Tully already took care of pulling them out. Maybe though the doc can neaten up Tully's efforts." Mitchell laughed, Willie laughed with him, and they walked on toward the doc's place, leaving behind a few stragglers who stared at the unlikely pairing and went on their own business muttering about folks not knowing their place.

The doc laughed too, which wasn't what Blue expected. "Mr. Mitchell, your method of taking out these stitches is not one I would normally suggest, but whoever hit you, and it looks like he got in a good many blows, was relatively accurate and only opened a few of the deeper areas of that slash. While you will have a scar, I doubt that your looks and charm will be compromised."

Blue figured the laugh was on target; "Well, Doc, you managed to insult and flatter me with the same words. That's a real skill, one I surely don't have."

Willie sat and listened and had no idea what the two men were talking on, but there wasn't nothing unnatural with what the doc was doing, washing out deep wounds with something smelled terrible, dabbing at small cuts on Mitchell's face, his hands, even lifting the ruined shirt to check the ribs. Damn but white men were blue-skinned, and this one had boot-sized bruises running up and down prominent ribs and across his belly.

He remained with Mitchell, seeing something flicker in the flat eyes that told Willie the man wasn't near as cheerful as he was mouthing off to the doc. It would be best that Willie stayed around so Mitchell he'd have a guide getting him back to that stall, then Willie could get to the bar, tell his story and earn a drink, never more than one, and have himself some fun with the boys who thought this Mitchell character was just another white man.

She came into their bed late when she had finished cleaning up after the children's attempts. They'd been so excited to eat outside, to make a pretty table under the elm tree, that she hadn't the heart to criticize their later attempts. They were tired, she said to Albert, they tried but their little hands were clumsy and she didn't want the added disruption of a broken plate, so first she put them to bed, and then cleaned up in the kitchen.

He reminded her that the girl came in the morning to do just that, clean up the evening's meal, the resulting stack of plates and flatware and pots used to prepare a fine dinner as always.

She smiled, leaned down and kissed him on the top of his head and he knew she was not in a romantic mood. He had learned to read her mood so that he did not impose his ardor on her inappropriately.

Their marriage had been a surprise; his beloved Dorothy actually enjoyed the physical side, a thought that never occurred to Albert during his first marriage. There had been little of the pleasant conjugal entanglements, and the one child created from those few times had died at birth, taking its mother with it.

In the back of his mind, that place where frightful thoughts stayed and were not meant to be examined, Albert knew that it was their visitor tonight who had awakened Dorothy to what was possible and right between man and woman. He had wanted, irrationally, to thank the man, but such words would be the height of ill manners. And although Mr. Mitchell was himself uncouth and poorly educated, his instincts would have immediately known and Albert would never have been forgiven for his indiscretion. In fact, he suspected that a sound thrashing would have been Mr. Mitchell's response to such impertinence.

Her body barely shifted his weight as she slipped in beside him. He let her settle, find the right place for the pillow beneath her head, move the sheet and light blanket where she wished it in this warm evening. The windows were open, he could hear the smallest rustle of the lace-edged linen as the cool air tried to penetrate the room.

He spoke while turned away, to allow her a certain emotional distance. "He is a stalwart man, Dorothy. You can see his fine qualities reflected in our son." He had practiced these simple words while she had been in the kitchen, picking each phrase to tell her without ever directly saying what he wished he could say.

Albert admired Blue Mitchell, was even admittedly jealous of the man in a distant way, jealous of what he'd had taken and received from his Dorothy, and yet he hoped, wished fervently, that his own physical attempts created the same response within his wife's flesh and soul. And he wanted so much to let her know that Robert, she had called him Robby when she put him to bed tonight and Albert quite liked the diminutive, the boy was their child, not just hers, not just sired by a man who could not live her life. It was an unfathomable and peculiar affinity between Mr. Mitchell and Dorothy that Albert could not hope to recreate on his own.

She rolled over, her warmth touching his back in those intimate places and she was crying as he had expected. Her hand rested on his shoulder, then slipped under his arm and it was all right when she whispered "Thank you." Then sighed, added 'dear' and her hand swept across his chest and he could roll over now and approach her after all.

"Mr. Mitchell, anyone associated with me or my racing stables does not brawl in the street, no matter the provocation." Belmont's face was red, his eyes wide and in Blue's estimation of such matters, the man's heart was overworked and stuttering, moved along with the expletives that Belmont did not use but were hidden in the gaps of breath between the words.

Blue didn't bother to tell the man it was none of his business how Blue led his life. He had a comment, though, and once spoken it seemed to make Belmont's temper rise. "No man beats on me and gets away with it. Let it happen and by god you're dead the next time."

The two glared at each other across the shined desk. Blue had been summoned to Belmont's office; the short note said that since he already knew the way there would be no car, no carriage and driver. It was a direct order to appear, and it took Blue a few minutes of thinking to decide.

Belmont wasn't his boss, but Con had loaned him out to the man and Blue'd agreed to it, so there was some reason to do as he was told. It went direct against his nature, but he'd given his word, which Con knew meant he'd honor the bargain.

For now he stood in front of the fancy desk, looking at the man posed by the window, glass pulled up, fresh air trying to mingle with the heated, human-thick air that got trapped in these damned high-storied buildings.

Yes it was time for him to get out, go home, but he had a few bits of unfinished business.

As usual Mitchell was disreputable, almost bad enough this time that the doorman was not going to let him inside until August actually went downstairs and vouched for the man.

It was all over another fight, the one that had been reported to August while tasting a good port at the sporting club. George Smith, only recently allowed admittance to the club simply because of his less-than-sterling sobriquet of 'Pittsburg Phil', was the bearer of the sordid tale. Despite the nickname, Mr. Smith was amassing a fortune through his betting practices, startling those who owned and raced horses, for most serious bettors did not in normal practice keep their winnings for any length of time.

Thus Mr. 'Pittsburgh Phil' had been allowed entrance into the club after much discussion and dissension. Almost his first conversation with August had been an argument against the outlandish cowboy who had accompanied Belmont's wonder colt East, and had been seen to challenge and come close to beating a man to death on the street. That he had later been seen in the company of Willie Simms, a Negro, and they were laughing together, that was another affront. Mr. Smith was of the opinion that such behavior reflected badly on those involved with racing. And he offered his opinion to August in a loud tone specifically designed to be overheard by the politely curious members.

August wanted to defend Mitchell by reminding those who were eavesdropping that he had known Mitchell for these few weeks and had come to the conclusion that the man would have a decent reason for his assault; then again it did not seem politic to insult Smith at their first encounter. Or to be forced into defending Blue. That too was an insult, that August Belmont's judgment of man could be challenged by such a brash newcomer.

In point of fact, August was enraged that Blue took to fighting in public. He had come to think on the man as a gentleman, and gentlemen fought within the boxing ring, with rules and a timekeeper; they did not brawl in the open streets.

It was truly peculiar that a person such as Blue Mitchell had found a place in August's world of bankers, railroad magnates and racehorse owners, those whose ideas were ahead of the times. And now here was cowboy behavior and actions that confounded August. He must have been fooled by his original impression, then later too sympathetic to the bruises and fresh stitches on Mitchell's face.

Blue broke into the silence; "I was told Curly runs a race in two days. His first race and I aim to stick around until then. To make sure nothing happens to him that might keep him from racing. Them fellas I went after last night, they got the reputation of trying to stop a good horse. And I know word's out on Curly's speed. With all the spying and nosing about, no way that could be kept a secret. Too many of those bums come out to see him run and check those watches they carry."

It was a lot of words for the usually reticent cowboy and August could see the effort in the eyes, a thinning of the lips. One hand, freshly bandaged and looking swollen, was wiped across the bruised mouth.

"Mr. Belmont, you pay me now, I'll be gone after that race, and when I finish some private business. I hear too that your trainer's coming to work soon. That's good news for Curly."

Never said, never spoken out loud, careful words well put but they did not blind or fool August. Mitchell and Bowdry's animosity toward each other had been visible from the first moment, and August held a suspicion that Bowdry was the last bit of 'business' Mitchell had to finish before taking his leave.

However, he chose to ignore what might befall Mr. Bowdry. There was no point in warning Mitchell away from the man, and deep inside where a civilized person did not venture, August knew that Bowdry was less than conscientious as a trainer, taking out his spite on the Connor Norris colt instead of confronting the man who enraged him, and Belmont preferred that any vengeance be applied by Mitchell, who had no reputation here to protect, and had already shown himself to be less than a killer but more than a well-mannered pugilist.

Bowdry would be punished, and perhaps August would keep him in his employ, on the understanding that his work would be restricted to supplies and employment of stable workers and he would never touch or give orders on a horse's care again.

With that highly contagious thought in mind, August Belmont turned and once again studied the face and form of the most unlikely person ever to be in his employ, and he had to smile. Mitchell returned the smile with the devilish grin that heightened his eyes to a molten color such as seen recently in the windows of Tiffany's in the City. There was complete understanding between the two men, without a word spoken beyond the first foolish statements.

He needed to get back to the now-familiar stall. Funny how quick a man took to a new home. He wondered if women did the same, or did they need specifics like walls and roofs and pretty curtains on the windows before it was home. He'd made camps and stayed two, three days and they'd been some of the best homes he'd ever had, beating out bunkhouses and back rooms, soft beds and pretty walls. He snorted; then again he weren't too particular most times, as long as it wasn't the inside of a jail.

There was one camp in particular, down near that Colorado mining town above the pass, but more east, in the limestone rocks and deep in a draw. Prettiest place, water running out of a crack in the rock, trees for shade, good grass for the horse. It was when he had the bay racehorse, a sweet mount; had the heart of a lion, never would quit in a race. Horse had been raced too much and needed to rest; Blue needed rest too.

He thought on where he'd ended up later, caught in the middle of a family feud. But that draw, with the water and grass, the call of an annoyed hawk registering its complaint that Blue'd taken up residence in his territory. He could sit and watch the bird fly, wing down and disappear, then climb up with a limp morsel caught in his beak.

His friend Peter Charley, he'd gone into that same draw to heal another horse. And himself. To get away from the whites, to find comfort with the silence and the wind. Blue shook his head, another dead man in his past. A man who'd gone to sleep one night and never woke up. Blue still used some of the man's gear, and never regretted turning loose the ugly, long-nosed pacing mustang Peter Charley favored.

His sigh was explosive; too far back, too many of them. He would leave here with respect for one or two of those he'd met, but no friends, nothing but a few memories added to his life.

Then August Belmont handed him a white envelope, stamped and shut. "There's your promised money, Mr. Mitchell. And I will be sure that Wilson makes a good reservation back to

Nebraska for you, on a sleeper car. You will not be traveling with a horse and sleeping on straw, not this time."

His heart lurched, his mouth went dry. He remembered a white envelope, her handwriting on the back with a torn address, his name on the front, with 'hand-deliver' printed in larger letters and underlined. He could see it, feel the thickness of the paper, not like this long and faceless envelope that might contain money but had little value compared to the few words of her note. He'd left it in the shirt he'd been wearing that had been pulled off him after the last fight. Another fight; goddman.

Blue nodded a quick 'thanks' to Belmont and hurried out of the office. This time he knew the way, and his legs moving quickly, head high, ribs sore but bearable; damn he remembered someone throwing away the ruined shirt. Damn it to hell that envelope had been in the front pocket; lost now to a street gutter or thrown in a trash heap, hidden under god knows what mess the human race could make with its garbage and waste and thrown-away clothing.

He recognized what his thoughts were doing to him, driving him out of this hellhole of people and noise and cars. He'd go one more time down to the ocean, and by god he'd shuck out of his shirt and boots and maybe find a pair of those soggy wool pants the men swam in, but no shirt, no foolish hat. Just him and the water and to hell with proper attire or behavior; man was born naked, and bathed naked, so he would swim and duck under and play in the ocean as he'd snorted and floated and even swum in any number of high-flowing rivers.

First he had to find the shirt, and the small square of envelope. He reached the stall, yanked on the door and bumped into Willie Simms trying to come through the door same time as Blue. "Here, Mister Blue Mitchell, I felt this in that rag you was almost wearing and considered you might be wanting what was in the pocket afore I threw it away."

The address was smudged, as was the front printing; both covered by a crusted stain. He took the envelope from

Willie, noting the shameless white paper against the dark of the jockey's hand.

"Thanks." Ah, not enough, nothing said or done could be enough. His son's home lived on the back of that small piece of paper. Willie cocked his head; "You are a strange one, Blue Mitchell, but I can trust you. Have to, you and me and Curly are the only ones who know."

Willie asked him to sit with the colt, they'd take turns, this close to a race and with the word getting out on the colt's speed, why now they couldn't leave Curly's good health to chance.

He sat himself outside Curly's stall and let the colt play with the top of his head, and they passed an hour, maybe more, until the colt got bored and went back to eating hay. Blue lay down, the raw side of his face toward the stars. He figured he was so damned uncomfortable he wouldn't sleep but he made a liar of himself and it was the odd sound of a boot crunching close to his ear that woke him.

He listened intently even as he kept his head on his arm, took to pretending and waited, concentrated on letting out small breaths as if he was still sleeping and he heard another crunch, a step. Sounded like two men.

When it seemed they were close enough, he rose quickly, pushed off the ground by fury. Two men all right, quick with a drawn knife, a set of those damned knuckles again. Blue grabbed the shovel he'd left close, swung it low, knowing to not aim for the head. The swing took one man down from the knee. Blue heard the cry, swung backhand and saw the second man duck, try to throw the knife in desperation and Blue laughed as the knife rang on the shovel blade, then bounced into piled manure.

The son of a bitch ran, leaving his buddy crawling, face drawn in intense pain. Damn but it was a familiar face, one of those several men had come to Tully's rescue and were turned back by their own crowd. Blue decided he truly hated this east coast, where there not enough room for a man to get away from his enemies.

Blue carefully put down the shovel out of reach of the wounded thug, and stood over the man who'd finally quit trying to crawl from his troubles. The man looked up, pleading his case before Blue even spoke.

"Mister, we was paid, it ain't personal, just want. . ." Then it crossed the twisted features that he was saying too much and Blue hadn't yet asked a question.

Blue nodded; "You was paid. Give me the man's name." He got what answer he expected. "Don't know, we never know. It comes through a note from a street kid. . ." Here the man stopped and Blue prodded him with a boot toe; "It comes through Tully's what you mean to say."

The man's relief was obvious; "Yes sir and Tully he got himself a broke jaw from that tussle with you. But he don't know neither. Gets a message and we just hit. Who we're told, don't know why. . ." The man quit again, staring up at Blue, seeing something that meant he was in deeper trouble.

NINETEEN

This was what he didn't understand. He'd come across it in Denver, Deadwood, once down in Tucson. Hired killers, trash willing to hurt, maim, even brutalize and kill a man they didn't know on account of money. He'd always thought, before he learned different, that the Army, it could be like that, men paid to slaughter. Then he'd met Josh Snow, and lived at the Fort and learned those men weren't killers, they were more likely trained to stop trouble. Despite a different way of seeing things, Blue had developed an admiration for the men who chose their life.

He stared at the man holding a smashed knee. "Looks to me your hired-out days're over, son. Blow like that to the knee takes a man down hard, and it don't knit and heal like ribs and jaws."

There was more to say, questions to ask but he didn't have the stomach for what it would take to drag a few more words out of this one. The rage building in him left a sour feel, like he was getting to be friends with brutality.

"You get up, best you can, and go on, mister. Tell that Tully, I'd write it down for him but I don't 'spect the man reads too well, tell him this colt's guarded safe and no point in taking cash for a job he can't do."

The leg was twisted at the wrong angle and the man grunted, then cried out in standing but Blue kept his distance, shook his head the smallest amount when the man glanced his way. He watched the son drag himself, leg hauled behind him, hurting like hell and he'd done that to the man. He didn't know his name or nothing 'bout him and it was all over running a clean horse in a legal race.

He slid down the wooden door, back to the boards, feet stretched out in front of him. A few new bruises, two men set on their heels and running like dogs. And a curious chestnut colt who once again arched his neck over the stall door and tugged on Blue's hair.

Hell, it was only a horse race.

Next morning, George Bowdry was in his office, Blue could see motion through the paned window, watched a shade or something pulled up, then dropped down. The boys were going through their chores, no hurry, doing nothing wrong. Blue was willing to bet Bowdry had expected a call to him, a running stable boy bringing bad news.

Willie brought him coffee, said the boys'd cooked up a mess of eggs, toasted some bread; if he was willing to eat with them they'd consider it an honor.

He stood, aching, eyes filled with sand. The coffee tasted good even without sweetening or canned milk and by god he was hungry. "Willie, two men. . ." Willie grinned, then turned his head. "I know, we know. Saw that man dragging himself out of here and we knows him, he's for cheap hire and it was you sleeping to the colt's stall so we didn't bother chasing him."

"Thanks, Willie, I'll be 'long directly."

He walked over to that single window and stood indecently close, like he'd done that one day with the chestnut colt sticking his head in Con's window, chewing on them dirty curtains and making everyone laugh. He was that close and just stood there. He could hear and almost feel Bowdry poking around, moving something, then a chair scratched on wood and it all went silent. As if the man, the room itself, didn't dare to breathe.

Blue spoke in a normal voice; there was no point letting Bowdry know how goddamn mad he was, for he had no proof that the orders sending Tully and kin came from this office. Blue had nothing but well-honed instincts, and he was learning that instinct had no value in this law-run place.

It was an effort to keep his voice even; "That colt came through the night just fine, he's out there now running light with Willie taking the reins. It should be a good race tomorrow." He took in his own breath, felt his broke fingers trying to curl into a fist. "Gonna be a fair race tomorrow. Mr. Bowdry."

He moved quietly away from the window; let the bastard sweat out how long he had to sit still and hold his breath.

From the slight rise he could see past the fencing to the track itself and it was easy picking out the colt. The stride, the copper coloring that had gotten richer as the colt grew up, the shape of the head, the rider crouched, legs drawn up into short stirrups, body balanced over the colt's back, shoulder over the colt's shoulder, butt over haunches, in complete, invisible harmony with the colt.

Again Blue admired Willie's hands, their connection with the colt's wet mouth through the bit, making suggestion, offering guidance. A whip lay in Willie's palm but when Willie made a move, giving Curly more rein and more'n likely squeezed with his ankles and calves, the colt took a longer stride and another until the legs were a blur and Blue could hear the wind, feel the excitement as if he were up on the chestnut's back. He tasted jealousy as he watched the colt run. Chances were Con Norris would never raise another one as good as this colt.

The flat-out didn't last long for it was only meant to give the colt a hint of tomorrow. It was a battle pulling up as Willie didn't want to haul on tender flesh so he sat his weight into that flat saddle and then half-stood and Blue let out his own breath as the colt slowed, trotted, then came to a walk, jittery and eager, but obedient to the skill of careful hands.

Damn the man could ride, and the race would be fair as a Nebraska cowboy with the help of some determined stable hands could make it.

There were other riders on the track, other horses laboring under their guidance; the short stirrup was the only seat they rode but it was easy picking out those who thought the idea foolish. Men whose hands were hard, elbows and shoulders one block of muscle and bone, legs tilted, pushing away from the horse's motion, riding against the speed.

He'd had work to do, papers to fill out about upcoming races where Mr. Belmont wanted his string of horses to run. It was almost time to declare for the Futurity at Sheepshead Bay. It was Mr. Belmont's fervent wish that one of his entries be the winner, and until that Mr. Franklin took over, it was George Bowdry who would make the choices.

His intense work, the shuffle of paper, the silence in his office, had nothing to do with the uncouth and unpleasant man who had decided to stand outside the shuttered window and shout out his threats and designs. This peculiar bit of business would be discussed with Mr. Belmont, before his good colt won the Futurity, after of course he won the Ben Brush Futurity tomorrow.

Brighton Beach track officials named the race after Ben Brush, Kentucky Derby winner and rising sire. Willie Simms had ridden the colt to that victory. This was the first running of the

Ben Brush, so it would be highly prestigious that a Belmont horse ridden by Simms won the coveted trophy.

All the eligible colts were entered, even the rough and sometimes unmanageable Nebraska chestnut. Willie Simms had asked to ride the colt, even when Bowdry wanted him on Tom, registered as Better Tomorrow, but it was the man's preference and Bowdry would not cross Willie. For all he was a Negro, and a jockey, he held a special place in Mr. Belmont's racing stable, having once ridden and won before the Queen.

It was a trying time, but soon enough he'd have the figures and facts in the correct columns, and he could dismiss the chestnut colt and put Willie back on the good horses where he belonged.

There was little noise outside the window, a bird's song, the rustle of those small bushes meant to give Bowdry some privacy. He risked a glance, raising the threaded shutter and the space was empty, the singing stopped; small birds flew up from the bush. The man was indeed gone.

He'd eaten the breakfast they'd cooked for him, later someone left a thick sandwich wrapped in a napkin on his bed for lunch, and now in the day's miserable heat, one of the stable boys approached him. Blue said his thank-you for the food, knowing these men were going out of their way to take care of him. He was learning it was risky for them, even as a group, to deal with a white man who was an outsider.

The man nodded, a quick head bob. "Mister Blue Mitchell, if you's inclined Willie said for me to sit here with this colt you both think so much on while you go sleep. 'Specting you'll be horse-setting again tonight."

Blue wanted to laugh; he was being babied for the first time in his life. "It's fine by me, if you don't mind. He likes playing with your fingers but he don't bite. Much." Blue grinned; the stable boy was startled then grinned back. "Leastways he ain't bit me yet. But you know 'bout horses like I do. Can't ever quite be sure what they'll do next." That head bob again, and the stable boy sat himself on a chair placed near the colt's stall for that very purpose.

"Have yourself a good sleep, Mr. Mitchell." Blue looked at him; "I don't know your name." "It's Marcus, Marcus Fever. Folks don't ask me so I don't bother to tell 'em." Blue stuck out his hand, "Nice to meet you, Mr. Fever. And rather than sleeping, think I'll take me a swim."

This time he knew exactly where the water was, and that a man could hire a pair of wool britches, change into his swim clothes in a slatted dressing room and make a run for the water so he didn't embarrasses himself that much. Or any such folk around him that were so delicate they couldn't see human flesh without suffering from the fantods or trembles.

By god he was tired and wouldn't mind a sleep 'bout now but he was here, to this place, only one more day and the water would wake him and become a memory he'd keep a long time. Water and the boy; two things he could never replace or visit again.

He took a dollar out of the padded envelope Mr. Belmont had given him. He didn't bother to count the bills but told Marcus that he was leaving the money, don't let Bowdry near the stall or the bed. Marcus nodded that quick one tilt and Blue knew his cash was safe.

The walk was familiar, tiring 'cause of the heat but the reward was waiting for him; he stopped, lifted his head, scented the wind. He'd learned to like that smell.

A man and a woman split and walked past him, the woman looking back as if he were a bug or a mangy dog and Blue had the grace to nod and not tease her with a grin or a flash of temper. She blushed anyway and hurried to keep up with her husband.

Whatever it was in him, times were he could come to hate himself and the devil that showed too quick and scared normal folk.

He walked slower, kept to the outside of the boardwalk and let folks pass without looking up. He'd never been this opened before. Cut in half and emptied out.

It cost twenty-five cents to rent a small room and one of them suits, it was worth it he decided. He barely listened to the strange little man who told him the rules, more rules; no running around on the beach, no showing off, go into the water for its beneficial healing powers, then return with decent haste to his assigned dressing room.

A lot of rules for the twenty-five cents handed over and Blue received a baggy, foul-smelling heft of wool that made him want to laugh. But he weren't going in there full-dressed again and risk his boots. He didn't have enough dignity left to lose his clothes too. So one of these eastern ideas of manly covering would have to do.

Itchy, too big, hanging down over his knees so he pulled the water-logged string tighter, glad he'd kept on his own under drawers, and he was ready to venture out of the small cabin. Ain't no way to call it a room, hell a man could barely turn around inside.

The wet sand felt good under his bared feet; he stood a moment, and let his toes curl until the sand under them give way, then harden. He took a step, looked back, and there was his footprint, wet and shiny. Then a curl of water, thin and chilling, swept over his feet and past him and the footprint was smeared, washed, pulled away and gone.

This time he walked into the water up to his chest, no hesitation, feeling the cold but liking it, challenged to keep his footing, pushed and pulled by water around his legs, thighs, even hugging at his waist.

He was laughing, coming up out of a white-rimmed break, when he realized a small child was splashing toward him, a boy, white haired, tanned, yelling as he fought the water and Blue leaned down, grabbed and held the boy, pulled him from the water high over Blue's own head, feeling water pour off the child's body, drenching his chest and shoulders. It was baptism like his own mama used to talk about. It hadn't worked for Blue, but this small being whose ribs felt like tree twigs, whose hair was his own, whose eyes belonged to the ocean, he baptized Blue with the waves.

"I told Mama we'd see you again and she said hush and go to sleep but I dreamed of you last night, I knew you were here."

The boy managed to wiggle around out of Blue's grasp and sat on his shoulders, riding high, letting Blue take the water's half force for them both.

He walked toward her, and the two girls, who had held back, dressed in their girl-child dainty version of a swimming costume, uneasy about putting their toes into the reaching water. He got close to her; then, embarrassed and too aware of how poorly he was dressed, Blue bent down and his son stepped off his unlikely horse, ran to his mama and chattered endlessly.

"Robby. I told you not to go in the water without me." Her voice was sharp, but Blue took in the change in name and he grinned at the woman and her three children.

Dorothy Marquardt's eyes were enormous. Blue felt more naked than he'd been in her bed. "Blue, your chest, your ribs, what's happened to you?" He shrugged; "Mostly bad tempers, ma'am."

He spoke their names to the girls and they giggled and he looked at their mother, not knowing what he could do. Robby tugged on his arm; "You're all cut and torn, like my old teddy bear."

Blue rested his hand on the boy's head, looked at the boy's mother and said 'goodbye' without speaking the words. He let the boy go and hurried past them to his torn clothes and broke-down boots and the thoughts of losing that boy and his mama forever.

They were gone when he was dressed and out of the stink in that small room, on wet sand again. He'd hurried too much, his boots rubbed on sandy skin. He was never coming back to this haunting place.

TWENTY

Marcus was setting in the chair at Curly's doorway when Blue returned. The water's momentary energy was gone but inside him a new wound had opened, and its chill wasn't going to leave.

Marcus spoke in a simple manner, telling Blue what he had guessed; "That Mr. Bowdry he come down here telling me to get on with my chores and I said I was doing what I was meant to do, and I would get to the sweeping and picking soon as time was right. He was some angry, Mr. Mitchell, but I didn't let him move me, I know what needs doing."

Blue went into the stall, got the thick envelope and took out a dollar but Marcus stood in the doorway and said it straight, looking Blue in the eye; "You offer me that money and I'll be offended, Mr. Mitchell. Willie and me and the others, we want that colt to have his fair chance. We ain't doing this for money. None of us likes Mr. Bowdry and his temper around the horses no sir."

Blue laughed, rubbed at his hair, feeling the dried salt. "Guess you put me in my place, Marcus." The man stepped back; "I didn't mean no disrespect." Blue realized he'd crossed an unseen line; "As long as the colt is doing fine, Marcus, and you forgive me for treating you wrong, then we're even." "It's all right by me, Mister Blue Mitchell."

Marcus grinned quickly, the serious business done, "That colt likes my fingertips too much but he ain't interested in my hair. Guess it might be hard for him to get hold of."

Both men laughed, the colt pushed his head over the door and Marcus touched the soft nose. "He's the best. We all got our money on him tomorrow."

Blue slept across the colt's stall door again, first setting in the chair, then finally lying down, the cut side of his face up, head supported on his arm. He wasn't aware when Marcus came by and dropped a blanket over him. The smell was familiar, horse sweat and wool, so it didn't set off Blue's senses.

He woke hungry and rested, with the colt nickering over the door at him, wanting breakfast and some attention. It was in the air, the sense of excitement; even Curly who'd never raced was feeling the edge.

The coffee and eggs that the stable boys laid out for him went down easy but then Blue's belly turned into mush and he wanted to get away, from the boys, the crowds coming in to the track, the whole goddamned world. It was early but they were there, bettors and travelers, ocean-going families and horse owners. They filled the stands, walked around the grounds, asked questions and had to be sent out of the shedrows so they didn't bother the horses.

Blue checked on the colt, found him lying down, legs curled under his chest, chewing disinterestedly on a few stalks of hay. Blue went in the stall, Curly looked at him without concern so Blue sat down, back to the wall. "Curly, it's just running. All them damn fools out there yelling, it don't mean a thing. You know you can outrun all the nags they got here, so go to it, kid."

It was foolish, childlike, an idiocy for a full-grown man to be setting on the floor of a stall talking to a horse. But he knew, deep inside where bad things got stored, that he was terrified and was talking to ease out that awful fear. The last race had been with Joshua on the good bay and Blue wasn't going to remember the day. Wasn't going to let today's race get to him. Even though it already had.

Like hell, he thought. He wasn't that smart or clever to ignore the still-fresh memory of the boy's face, her son's face, and a brave horse trying his best. They were dug into him, memory burned deep and permanent. The fall he'd barely seen, the death held in his arms.

Willie startled both Blue and the colt, who scrambled to his feet as Blue came up and they collided, Blue ending up hanging on to the colt's neck.

Willie laughed, then sobered. "It's getting that time Mr. Blue Mitchell, that your boy here has his chance to show what he can do. I'll be riding him, don't you worry, Curly and I we talked over what has to be done."

Blue left Curly to Willie and Marcus; they knew the system, the way things were; they understood the racetrack and all its special rules and regulations. He knew he lived in the stall and was allowed some freedoms only because of Belmont's money, so he wouldn't risk hurting Curly or no one else, by getting in the way.

And if he saw Bowdry, well it wasn't the time. He'd studied on that need while he talked to Curly. But the time was coming. After the finish of Curly's first race, though, he'd have no bonds keeping him in check.

Seven races, each set to go at their own time. Precise and orderly and Blue wanted to get the hell out of this life. He'd stand a few more hours, then he'd find a train going west and be satisfied.

He stayed to the rail, near the shedrow, where he wouldn't see or be seen by the Marquardt family. Yesterday, holding the boy, his son, had knocked him sideways. He couldn't let the boy into his life. It wasn't right for the kid, or his momma, or any of them, but mostly her. Mrs. Albert Marquardt. It would be wise to say that name full and out loud when he got to remembering, wishing, aching for what he didn't have. Hell of a mess for a cowboy bronc buster and all 'round drifter to be in love with another man's wife and to have sired another man's child.

His temper got to him then and he spun around, went back to the shedrow and stalls where he planned on beating the hell out of the wood walls, and walked in to a scrawny son of a bitch digging through the sad facts of Blue's life.

He decided he wasn't going to fight again, he was getting close to a record of too many fights in too few days so he bellowed and the little fella jumped a few feet, dollar bills and a filthy shirt, the white envelope, scattered out of his hand.

Two men, one a good foot taller than the other, stared at their opponent. Blue shook his head; "Now there, it ain't polite to rob a man of what little he's got. You can do better in that crowd out there, I figure those hands of yours can slip in and out of pockets real easy. So you got told to come here, do this 'cause you was ordered and sure as hell not for the ready money. You wouldn't know I got paid yesterday, or even was living here. Only a few folks know 'bout that."

The man was trembling, water collecting at the corners of his mouth, dripping off his nose even; Blue reckoned he'd never seen a poorer specimen of human kind before. With that graying brown hair and the tiny eyes, he was kinda like a rat on hind legs.

"Son, you turn those pockets out for me." Any man wearing a coat in this weather had to be using the pockets. Then he laughed, it was the coat Belmont had bought for him in trying to make Blue a gentleman. But it sure wasn't the same old man he'd given it to after the fine meal.

Hands trembling, once getting caught in a sleeve lining, the man shrugged out of the stained coat, held it by the filthy collar, shook it and nothing rattled. Blue didn't take this as enough. "Pockets, inside and out so's I can see." Sure 'nough, a few dollar bills rolled out but nothing else. He'd kept an eye on the envelope when he'd first scared the son and it was still on the floor at other side of the bed. The flap was open, a few bills had been pulled part way out.

"Those're my dollars you son of a bitch." He let the edge come into the words and the rat took two steps backwards, pulled a few more dollars out of his pants. "Here, you can have these but I didn't take them from you. Just don't hit me."

Well that does it, Blue thought; his taking down of Tully had proved useful after all.

In the background, outside in a different world, there were cheers and yelling and a great whooping roar and a race had been won, most likely by the favorite.

"Mister, you keep what's in your pocket, you're too flea-bitten for me. I'll keep what belongs to me and nothing more. Now get!" He stepped back and that little man he sure could run from a standing start.

It took maybe two minutes to pick up everything, only then did it occur to Blue that he best count the money and put it in his pocket where he had some chance of protecting it.

Two hundred dollars. That felt odd, it didn't seem, with all Belmont's millions, that the trip and the having to live in this hell hole racetrack was worth the effort. Not for two hundred dollars, but he'd take it, and the train ticket home, and be shut of the Easterners and their strange ways. He folded the money and stuffed it back into the envelope, which he buttoned in the pocket of the cleanest shirt he could find. He'd leave this place with some bits of him left whole.

It didn't come natural to him, to fret about the amount of money paid out for his work. He'd taken five dollars from a scruffy rancher for riding down a paint colt. Five dollars was what the man could afford and Blue'd been honored that he got paid at all. Guess it was the dimensions of Belmont's reputation and wealth that poked a greedy hole in Blue's normal business dealings. For that moment, he didn't much like what he'd become.

He stepped out of the stall, hesitated, then walked toward the grandstands and all the yelling.

They were racing again, maybe ten horses running too close to the rail, pushing each other, legs flying fast enough you couldn't count them, white socks and black hooves, red, brown, dark gray bodies, bright colors and black tails; not like racing with the Indians, where the wide plains was the course and there weren't turns or yelling bettors standing on high layered seats but full out, each running their separate course.

Here it was a different race but still. . .his gut turned, his hands got sweaty. Inside this madhouse Curly would run with no way to avoid a spill in front of him, no possible freedom, just a bunched mass running for their lives. This was how the course had been set at the Fort. . .Blue shook his head. No. He was across the country and these were professional jockeys.

He saw the winner fly past a high white pole and people in the stands cursed, tore up papers, looked at each other in disgust. A few bettors cheered in separate corners. The favorite didn't win.

Then it was Willie thrown up on Curly's back, feet tucked high into the small iron stirrups, the flat seat of polished leather where he sat was hardly enough to call a saddle. It was Bowdry holding Curly's bridle, talking up at Willie Simms, whose dark face was stilled, mouth set, looking down and nodding, not saying a word. Blue got in closer, heard orders he didn't like; "We want you in behind the leaders on the rail so the colt has a chance at the end. We know it has stamina, but a turn of speed, that's not a certainty. So you will stay up with the leaders."

Man didn't know the horse at all, damn him. Willie nodded to Bowdry's head as the man slammed his bowler hat on, spooking Curly who half-reared and came down and must of caught Bowdry's foot for he cursed and raised a hand and Willie's voice cut through the noise.

It wasn't the way a Negro talked to his boss but Willie was riled; "Mister Bowdry you touch this horse and I'll by god run you over." Plain as could be said and Bowdry turned, pushed through a growing crowd, left Willie on the colt to get himself out onto the track.

Willie saw Blue and smiled, did that quick head-bob and Blue came through the people pushing in too close. He knew Curly was going to rear, could see it in the white-rimmed eye even before a child ran too close. The colt backstepped as he reared and Willie slid off, the colt stayed too high too long until

Blue half-jumped and grabbed a rein, spoke the colt's name and Curly came down, landing hard on his front legs, snorting, shivering as Blue touched his neck, stroked the wet muzzle. He told the colt it was all right, fine now, these folks meant him no harm.

Willie appeared at Blue's elbow. The men studied each other; Willie's face was dusty, he had a small cut on his neck. Blue bent down, grabbed Willie's knee and toss him up on Curly. A few touches with his hands, a light feel of the reins and the colt bowed his neck, knowing now exactly what waited for him.

Blue pushed himself to the rail, held his breath until he felt he was seeing spots and dancing lights, then forced himself to catch a good breath, even pulled in some of the salt air, and tried to laugh at his nerves. It was only a horse race and he wasn't riding.

The colt started about mid-pack in a ragged line held only by a starter's glare. At the signal, a mass of horses bolted, barely contained by their riders. Two colts were half sideways at the start, one staggered and fell close to Curly, who jumped the downed colt's head and the entire parcel of folk to the stand groaned, gasp, one woman even cried out but Curly knew what he was doing. Running the Nebraska sand hills made any racecourse easy.

Willie let the colt run against orders to the outside, up with the four horses tight-bunched on the rail. Curly was moving light and smooth; Blue knew as if he was aboard the colt. He grinned and pounded on the wood fence and the man squeezed in next to him said 'you know something I need to know?' but Blue didn't hear him.

Cheers came for several horses, names Blue recognized from daily workouts, horses that were nothing next to Curly's waiting speed. A few of the leaders dropped back, one bay was struggling and Blue had a bad feeling. But Curly was safe and out of the pack, still on the high long side of the track, running smooth. The bay stumbled, the jockey went over his head and instead of running on with the herd, the bay came to a slow three-legged walk and Blue's belly turned on him. Blood ran down a white-stockinged leg, a wound from running too close, steel shod, cramped together. Damn.

That high-poled white line was coming up quick, with Curly still two horses outside and behind the leader, a big gray that Blue remembered. He'd watched that colt run out of control on the workouts, the jockey leaning back and pulling. Now that jock was rolled forward, reins too long and the gray was going full out, his powerful rhythm uneven.

Then Blue saw it, what he was waiting on, nervous, wishing hard, knowing that Willie knew, Willie could tell when it was right. Willie's hands went forward an inch, his legs tightened; the colt's ears came back as his neck lengthened, then his body sank down, his hind legs came up under his belly and Blue swore he could hear Willie laugh as the chestnut colt from Nebraska reached the laboring gray. It was almost done when the gray swerved, bumping Curly who was pulled up by Willie Simms for a step, then the chestnut colt leaped forward, crossed that finish line with the gray a short half-stride ahead.

Blue groaned, slapped the rail and the man next to him gloated; "You see, the gray's a better horse, Owned by one of the Dwyer brothers, they always got winners." Blue spun on the man; "You call swerving in front of a horse and bumping him off the winning line a victory. Hell, mister, they cheated right there in front of your face, they cheated a good colt and you think they have the best horse. Goddamn."

The man grinned; "Well mister, I had money on the gray, was told he'd win. Don't matter how, I got a parcel of coin coming to me from placing that bet."

It was difficult to breathe; Blue clenched his fists so hard they hurt. The man shrugged and shook his head; "See ya, mister. Got to go pick up my winnings.

There was a ceremony of course, that no one wanted to watch. A gray colt, lathered and shaking, stood held by two men with hard hands and wicked grins. A fat-bellied man accepted the trophy, a silver-plated bowl covered with leaves and vines and cherubs, though Blue didn't know what the half-naked babies were called.

Blue saw the important faces; Belmont's disgust was evident, Willie couldn't look no one in the eye and the damned trainer kept muttering about the importance of following his orders. Blue was tempted to hit the man but it wouldn't do no good.

They'd lost by being cheated; Belmont shook himself. "Willie, you and Blue take the colt back to the shedrow. Bowdry, be quiet."

A man gave a speech before he handed the big silver bowl meant for the winning owner to the crook who paid for the victory and was given what he didn't deserve. Those around him applauded and the Belmont staff scowled as they led Curly away.

Blue slid out of the line of folks, knowing he had no business there. Even Belmont frowned and the look on Bowdry's face was pure fury. Belmont took a few steps, then turned back. His voice was deadly calm; "I am going to have a talk with a few officials." He looked at each man, even at Marcus Fever, very carefully. "None of you will speak out of turn or cause any trouble." Then he walked away, in measured steps, back rigid, and Blue had a sense he wouldn't want to be sitting in the room when Mr. August Belmont Junior made his thoughts know.

Willie'd gotten off the colt and Marcus was holding Curly; both men were silent as they loosened the girth and Willie took the reins while Marcus bent down and smoothed each one of Curley's legs. Bowdry approached the two men. Blue stopped, not too close, just waiting.

"You didn't ride to my orders." Bowdry's voice held a growl but the words came evenly in a steady tone. Facts, not anger. Impressive for such a small-minded son of a bitch, Blue thought.

Blue moved, just a step or two, not closer to Bowdry and Willie but sort of sideways, maybe as a reminder. Bowdry glanced up and saw him; Blue grinned, tipped the edge of his hat. And knew to stay where he was.

Willie was ahead of the lecture; "Mr. Bowdry, Mr. Belmont he told me ever time I ride a race exactly what to do, him and his head trainer and now you, and I go ahead and ride like it feels the horse wants to be ridden and I won me awards and titles and got a good record of wins so I'll ride this here colt just like he wants me to ride him. Mr. Belmont he said nothing but I done the best could be done with that play and Mr. Belmont he told me I done right. Colt ain't hurt, I got him quick out of the way so his legs are clean. Mr. Belmont he will set things to order. He's a steward of The Jockey Club, and they won't take kindly to how the race was won."

Bowdry took a half step toward the jockey, Blue coughed and Bowdry spun on his heel, got himself together and started walking toward the office, where he worked and plotted. The building sat on a rise so he could see the exact limits of his small world.

TWENTY-ONE

Blue helped with putting away the colt, doing whatever Marcus and Willie asked, at ease with the excited colt, letting his hands touch and soothe until Curly breathed out a deep sigh and rubbed his head against Blue's chest.

Marcus spoke up; "That there colt knows you, Mr. Mitchell, what we going to do when you're gone?" Blue looked at the stable hand; "He's a good youngster, as honest as they come. Give him time, come in and brush him. He likes Willie riding him, and it won't take you long to make the colt a good friend. He's eager, and excitable, but a few more races and he'll figure out what he's supposed to do."

Blue stopped, rubbed his jaw which ached like he'd been punched hard. "What happened today says cheating may win but that colt, and you, Willie, you both got the heart. He checked when you asked him and then he ran hard enough to almost get there. Usually the horse quits when he's pulled up, or fights so that he gets in trouble. Belmont knows. He saw what I saw."

Silence ended the talk, anger seeped into each of the men; what had been done to a good horse was no surprise but it was wrong. Then Willie spoke up, with Marcus nodding in agreement.

"Ain't no way we can get you to staying, Mr. Mitchell? A few more days maybe? That Futurity, it's coming up soon, and it's on a nicer track and Bowdry'll be gone by then. Your colt, he's got him a good chance of winning some money. Big money. Those that cheated by God they won't be racing soon. Mr. Belmont he will make sure of that."

Blue cocked his head, stared at the small, dark men, men he'd never have known if he hadn't come East. He'd heard cowhands and drifters and soldiers sit and badmouth Negroes, especially up to the Fort when the buffalo soldiers got stationed there. Yeah they were different to look at, but in these two men at least, the love of horses, their skills with them, meant that the look and the eyes, the hair, were nothing. To them Blue was outlandish and it was simply how he come into the world.

No one couldn't fault a man for how he was born, only for what he did with the little he had. Blue figured he had too many times not done right, and too few times he'd done his own way against what those who were supposed to know demanded of him, and maybe that too was wrong.

"I thank you, Willie, and you too, Marcus, for the invite but I got to get some hard dirt and good grass under my feet, and a cow horse knows how to take the miles. This here sand and those wood boards you walk on, well the sand might do well on a race horse's legs but it sure grinds its way into a man's soul."

The world-famous jockey and an unknown stable hand looked at each other and grinned. Marcus told him the truth; "We had us a bet, no losers, just us two as winners, that you'd say almost 'xactly them words. You run yourself true to form, Mr. Mitchell, just like that colt you trained."

Blue countered; "You two still won't use my name and I ain't mister to no one. Makes me feel like I'm on the outside, where I usually am. I thought we'd come to an understanding but I guess not. Anyway, thanks for the invite." Here he looked at each man. "Mr. Simms, Mr. Fever, you take good care of that colt. I've got some unfinished business pressing on me and then I'll be leaving."

He didn't know if they were angry, insulted, or just plain amused by his speech but he'd wanted to tell them and didn't know another way. He knew he was no gentleman and only those with manners and good sense got called mister. To most of the world, he was 'Blue-Mitchell-that-son-of-a bitch', like they were all one word.

The two men nodded to Blue, then Marcus grabbed up a brush, tested it on his own hand to know it was soft, and began brushing the sweaty chestnut coat. Curly raised his head and stuck out his quivering lip in pure horse enjoyment.

Blue left the stall, stood outside the door a moment, checking on his surroundings.

A small man in a neatly tailored suit was walking down a shedrow and the men working with the colts all seemed to turn and half-bow to him so Blue guessed it was the new head trainer, the famous and well-respected Edward Franklin. Which meant he had only a few moments to get up to the office set on its bump called a hill and have a few social and polite words with the son of a bitch gentleman who thought he still ruled there. Bowdry might have manners and be able to add up figures, but to Blue it didn't work. Any man who used an animal cruelly to get some kind of revenge, he wasn't no better'n a damned skunk.

Daylight was slowly turning to dusk, a quiet time in the stables. The racing done, behind him in the stalls the horses ate their evening meal whether they'd earned it or not. The stable hands finished grooming, sat in a small circle cleaning up saddles and bridles, checking stitches and talking over how each horse had run, who'd done their best, who quit and why. Shedrow talk, where bets were made, horses discussed and dismissed, the winners getting most of the approval but there was always one man who said his colt or filly'd come in just behind the leaders, looking better with each race, gonna be a winner soon. Tonight the talk would also be about being cheated right to their faces and in front of a thousand people.

They kept on with their talk about men and horses and who could run, who quit when it got tough. Same discussion about both animals; neither good nor bad but what their hearts offered when called on for the impossible.

Three more steps and Blue stood at the office door, thought about knocking but hell he wasn't a gentleman, didn't have those useless restrictions holding him. He'd seen that dog kicked out onto the track to scare Curly, he'd heard the instructions given which would have maybe hurt the colt like that bay'd been hurt. The man needed to learn about being honest and doing the best he could, not sneaking around folks and cheating them to feed his self.

Bowdry heard him this time and stood behind his desk, holding tight to a raised pistol; his knuckles were white, his face cleared of all color. Blue studied the man, seeing the tremble in that tight hand, the quivering at the corners of the mouth. To Blue, it looked like the man might burst out crying and Blue briefly considered that Bowdry might have enough nerve to shoot.

A long moment, then Blue shook his head and entered the office, stood about five feet from Bowdry and his fiercesome pistol. The feist had been lying at his master's feet; the small dog stood, stretched, eyed Blue and only then decided to bark. The noise was less than threatening; Blue took a quick step toward the animal, who chose to sit down and busy himself cleaning after his nap.

"Mr. Bowdry, I come in here to get a few things straight. Figured I'd grab you by the balls and pecker and tell you what needs redoing in your life. But hell, man, I'm betting those balls and pecker're so small I'd never be able to find them."

Bowdry's face went even whiter, the eyes grew large, then squinted but there was no movement on that trigger finger. Blue wiped his mouth; "See, I was right, you ain't got any balls or you'd a shot me by now." Bowdry quivered, but still did nothing.

Blue reached across the desk and squeezed Bowdry's nose hard, until the man cried out and the pistol fell out of his hand, clattered on the desk, making Blue flinch as he twisted and held on to the nose. "Always suspicioned this was bigger than your pecker. You're getting back some on that beating you paid Tully for. No I ain't got proof and if I did don't think I'd take it to the law. You're the one I want learning the lesson. You want a man hurt, you hurt him yourself. Face-to-face." He pulled the nose sideways even harder.

Holding on gently now, just barely pinching when Bowdry tried to move from Blue's hand, he went on with his lecture. Then Blue laughed; it might be if the schoolmaster when he was growing up used such a hold, Blue could have learned more than how to write a few words, and how to read only if he struggled through it. It'd been his ma did most of the teaching.

"Now Mr. Bowdry, what you're feeling ain't nothing like what those boys did to me. And they paid. I figured you needed to pay out too." He gave one last yank, watched the man's eyes tear up, felt his mouth tremble under Blue's hand, and began to feel ashamed of his own bullying.

He released his grip and eased back from the desk, not bothering to pick up the pistol. He only had to glare at Bowdry when the man's hand tried to move and Bowdry pulled back, held his arms across his belly.

"You need to know, Mister Bowdry, that horses ain't humans and they can't fight back 'cepting for rebellion and then men like you hit them and call them renegades. You're the renegade here, hating me so you take out that hatred on a colt only wants to do his job. I can see why Belmont he decided to hire on a new man to train the stock. You ain't got the sense or kindness to deal with an animal as willing and fearful as a horse. You'd overrun the good ones and terrify the bad ones and hell the man'd lose his shirt right in public and folks would know it was you.

"If you were me and thank god that ain't happening, I'd be thankful to have a job ordering supplies instead of putting your name out there as trainer and doing as bad as only you could do. Them's my words of wisdom, Mister Bowdry."

He turned and put his hand on the door to open it and the pistol fired and Blue heard the sound, knew he'd made a fatal mistake, cursed under his breath and was grinning the same time that bullet hit him high in the hip. As he went down his thoughts were foolish; "By god I'm rump-shot."

Voices and feet and men running, a loud yell, and it was Willie Simms he recognized first. He couldn't get up, couldn't make his own feet work but he was awake and the damned wound stung, made him want to rub his backside but that seemed wrong with so much company showing up for the shooting. That damned dog was close to him, down on its front end, tail wagging, as if trying to get Blue to play. He wanted to yell at the dog that this was no time for games.

Instead he rolled onto his unwounded side and the dog disappeared as Blue looked for Bowdry and the man was setting down, something Blue wouldn't be doing for quite a while. Face wrinkled and tight, the pistol lay on the floor in front of the desk, stinking of powder, thin smoke curling upward; damn but Blue had broken a tried and true-given law; don't turn your back on an armed man. He just didn't think Bowdry had the balls.

Willie bent down, Marcus behind him; "You all right, Blue?" Blue grinned; "You know, if you'd called me Blue earlier maybe I wouldn't of got my ass shot off." Willie sank back on his heels and gave it right back; "You know, I don't think that figures right."

Blue couldn't resist; "Why not?" "You said you had business with Mr. Bowdry and I'm betting with Marcus it was you and your words got your behind shot, not us trying to be polite and respectful."

Marcus had his own point of view; "Now from what I'm seeing, mister. . .ah, Blue, you got a mild crease cross the top of your skinny rump and it won't be a day or two for when you sit down, you don't say some curse word intended for Mr. Bowdry here. Think he might just have lost his job and all you got was a little ole spot of blood. Hell man, I seen you trying to wash and you got more scars that tell a long tale. This one, why it won't be worth noticing, 'cepting maybe to a lady or two."

A lot of words, Blue thought, then he decided he'd stand up 'cause the boots he was looking at now were polished and fitted and he had a suspicion whose feet were stuck in them. Behind him a similar pair of boots belonged to that new trainer.

He kind of thought maybe if Bowdry's shot killed him, the man would finally have a decent reputation as a tough man to cross. The wound would be in the back, though, and that kind of shot never gave a man's rep much of a boost.

Getting up wasn't what Blue would call fun, holding on to the door, having Marcus push at him, then a clean white hand came down, a surprisingly strong hand that tugged and pulled and Blue was standing.

Blood ran down his pant's leg, into his boot, wet, chilled now, and his body was cold, his mouth dry. He turned slowly, leaning once on Willie again, then staring across the desk to study George Bowdry.

"Mister Bowdry, when you grow a set, be more polite to let a man know you're going to do something with 'em. It ain't right, shooting me in the backside, but I give you the try, it surely got my attention. Still it don't change my message to you, you treat them horses better or I'll come back with my own pistol. Then we'll see how you do shooting a man where he sits while he's facing you."

He nodded once to Mr. August Belmont, nodded again to the man he figured was Franklin and walked out of the office, limping maybe more than walking. Still it was under his own doing. He turned to Willie as Marcus came 'long to his other side. "That doc I've been seeing, you two'll help me get to his place again?"

He got a good scolding and something powerful and rude poured into the wound, no digging 'round for a bullet, not enough flesh cut into that he needed stitches. Just across the round beginning of his backside; from the front it would have hit a hip bone, or even bounced up to a rib. The doc told him while he didn't have much padding there, he had enough to keep the errant bullet from hitting anything vital. Blue disagreed, said that his sitting parts were pretty damned necessary for his line of work. And what the hell did errant mean?

Belmont was waiting for him when Blue got to the stall. It was night, late he figured, since he'd lost track of time. He didn't own one of those watches and usually time didn't matter. Cattle and horses didn't much care.

"Mr. Mitchell!" Still full of pompous indignation and Blue grinned. He was about to get fired so he spoke his piece first.

"Mr. Belmont. That Bowdry needs to learn manners. The few words I said to him weren't worth shooting me in the back." Belmont looked hard at Blue, cocked his head, seemed to be laughing suddenly. "Don't you mean the buttocks, Mr. Mitchell?"

"Well it's the back side of my front however you say it. Mr. Belmont. And it ain't going to make setting on a horse too easy for while."

"Mr. Mitchell, are you still intent on returning to Nebraska and Mr. Norris' employ?" Blue nodded, "That was the deal." Belmont rubbed his jaw, coughed politely into his hand and shook his head. "Now is there any way in which I can induce you to remain here? I'd like you to work with the horses, under Mr. Franklin of course as head trainer. He has the racehorse experience, but you seem to have. . .ah you have a certain touch in starting the youngsters. That colt has been a joy since he followed you off the train."

Blue was surprised, thought to sit down and got half way to landing on a heavy trunk before the crease reminded him so he grabbed the door to the stall and stood again.

"I take that as a compliment, Mr. Belmont. But me and the East, we don't see eye to eye on most matters. I will make you a promise, though. If Con Norris breeds another colt close to Curly in heart and speed, I'll make certain sure Con gets him to you well-started and ready to run. Best I can do. Mr. Belmont, sir." He actually nodded his head quick and Belmont seemed pleased.

There had to be something else; Blue's breathing was shallow, as if too large a gulp of air might hide the words Belmont would have to say. "That is more than I expected, Mr. Mitchell. Believe me, it has been a pleasure. A most peculiar pleasure but indeed a great experience."

Then there was a moment, time suspended, where Belmont struggled; "I have spoken at length with the race officials and The Jockey Club. There will be no repeat of what happened at the track, at least for the next few races. This was given as a solemn promise, and I believe these men, as they control what can happen on these tracks."

Both men sighed, Belmont offered his hand, Blue shook it carefully and they parted, Belmont to his offices, Blue to the shedrow where he'd had a temporary home.

Blue made a deal with the ticket man; there'd be a place on a load of furniture going west through Chicago Blue could have

William A. Luckey

and the fancy ticket Belmont had left as a parting gift got traded in for meals, water, and no one bothering him. Setting up looking out the window wasn't a good place to be right now.

He got on the train in the dark, midnight or somewhere close to it. All his gear, a few new shirts and those half boots that were comfortable now, beat up and even blood-stained but good enough to get him home. This time he was going home with more than he'd had.

He wadded up the straw, pushed himself inside on his good hip until he was comfortable, and lay there waiting for the lurch and clatter that told him he was moving on.

It come to him after an hour's ride, with the jerking and rattle of traveling, it came to him raw and hard that he would never see his son again.

A few days to Chicago, with stops where he got out, walked around, tried to wash up in whatever water he could get. Damned cold, splashing down on him from a hand pump to a long hose, cold but it felt good, his stench bound up in the straw and the single bucket, the hours of being shut inside.

They had a long stop in a little town west of Chicago, long enough that Blue got out of the box car, hanging on to the door and gently lowering himself to the ground. He walked, slow at first, stiff and uneven. After a few minutes, he could move easily, and found himself a small place where they served bad coffee and hard biscuits to the yard workers. No one looked up at him; the lady behind the counter took his order and paid no attention to his battered appearance. Busted-up old men like him might be invisible in the West; in the East he'd felt like a side show.

Back on the train, he settled into the straw bed he'd fashioned to fit his wounded flesh, and lay there, listening, hearing the rhythm and feeling as if everything he knew had disappeared, with nothing strong and clean to take its place.

TWENTY-TWO

He knew by the screaming brakes, the desperate push and pull of the car, hard enough to shuffle the crated furniture closer to him; the train was coming in for a big stop, a long hard grinding of parts and brakes that slowed this monster to a desperate whoa.

It would be North Platte, Nebraska. This time the train crew opened the sliding doors and let down a ramp so Blue could exit without a limp, no twinge in his backside from trying to swing down off the train couplings. It was North Platte; even where they stopped was familiar to him. Exactly where he and Rhynes had ridden in on the nervous colt and the good roan.

He hurried to pack his gear, stuffed it in a sack; now it dragged behind him, leaving a dusty trail, but he wanted off the infernal machine that ground into his life and took his breath.

What kind of horse would Con have sent to the small livery about two blocks from the train stop? Blue was guessing that Con and Belmont had been talking, either by telegraph or that new thing called the telephone. So there was hope the horse hadn't been setting and waiting for weeks. Blue didn't figure his backside was ready yet to ride out a stall-bound bronc.

The trainman, changed over in Chicago, stepped up to Blue. "Mister, I got word here for you." Blue got handed a small folded square, too close to that white envelope he had buttoned in his pocket; memory made him step back, hand fallen to his side. "It ain't going to bite, Mr. Mitchell. Guess it's from Con Norris up to Valentine. You best read it."

A telegram for him. Hell of a greeting to coming home. He dropped his gear, noting absently that if he was traveling horseback he'd best pack more closely or he'd leave a trail of ragged clothes and a few personal items littering the prairies the way those Easterners littered their own ground.

'Mr. Belmont wired two thousand in your name to the bank in Valentine.'

Blue shook his head in wonderment. Then he kept reading. The number was unreal to him, he'd think about it later.

'Right and the lady nurse got married July 18th. They're living to the house, Right's running the whole show.'

That was enough to take in, like a blow, soft and expected yet the words made the notion real. Good for Right, he thought, she was a strong thing for being small and young, and a woman. She'd get Right going in a better direction.

A few last words added on: 'You've got Sully to ride in. Curly's new half brother is a pistol.' It was a long speech and each letter cost; for once Con wasn't being close with his money.

Not there in the hand-set words, but in the direction of the information was the sentiment; welcome home.

It was the red roan, stout, calm in the eye, common-headed yet a good going and doing horse. Con had made arrangements with the hostler; Blue's gear was waiting, and even had been cleaned, with a new saddle blanket, a pair of empty saddlebags. The roan had been turned out daily, sir, said the hostler. Con's orders and out here Con Norris was as big a man as August Belmont back in New York.

It was late afternoon and the hostler suggested a good boarding house for the night; the woman cooked a fine meal, the beds were clean and a man needn't share with a drummer or any one of those scoundrels. He'd put in a word for him, the hostler said, if Blue wanted a good night's sleep.

Blue shook his head; he'd lived long enough in other folks' beds, he wanted his own now. So he spent a few minutes stuffing clothes and such into the saddlebags, and went to beg a fletch of bacon, the makings for coffee, from the hostler. Telling the man to put it on Con's bill.

Hostler laughed and said Con had sent extra, and gave Blue a new coffee pot, a small fry pan and even a sack of biscuits along with the bacon. "My woman made 'em fresh this morning. Mr. Norris he told us you'd come in today and would want to be going on." The man hesitated, rubbed his serious chin whiskers. "Now if it were me, I'd want a bath and a good meal, a soft bed, before any such ride."

The hostler studied Blue for a reaction; when he got nothing, no interest in being sent to a particular boarding house or hotel, the man turned away in disgust. His march through the livery ended up in a small, dust-ridden office, with him setting to a desk and writing down important numbers and letters in a thick book meant just for that purpose.

Blue had to laugh; Con knew him, he'd been riding for the man long enough Con knew all the flaws and troubles that hunted him and still kept him on the payroll. Blue stopped for a moment in his efforts to repack tight and neat; kneeling in the straw and manure-covered aisle of the cramped livery barn felt like a prayer to coming home.

He took the time to let the roan run some in a small round corral, let the range horse get some kinks out 'cause he wasn't use to standing in a stall for hours at a time. The roan was no disappointment; head down, tail up, bucking and bellowing like a good Norris-bred ranch horse and Blue had his doubts about riding the horse even when he got those bucks out of his system. Damn but his backside hurt just watching the roan sunfish and then settle into a gallop, hitting the fence once, backing off into another bucking spell before turning and trotting up to where Blue stood as if the past few minutes had been nothing but a breath of good air.

Blue put the bridle on that common head and led the sweaty horse to a hitching post. There he worked over the roan, letting his fingers feel for bumps and sore spots, touching the horse in a way that told ole Sully Blue was something familiar, nothing new.

There was a small cut on the heel bulb, fresh blood, not enough to slow the trip, but he went inside and got some of that tar, smeared it on the cut. Be good enough until they got home.

Brushed, saddled, bridle fitted to the coarse head, Blue loaded his meager gear behind the saddle, tied everything hard and tight, checked the cinch and then spent a few moments talking to the horse, telling him that for him, Blue, setting down in the saddle wasn't a simple matter and he hoped Sully would take it easy on an old man beaten half to death by those city folk.

Then he led the horse out into the sunshine, stuck a foot in the stirrup, slid up into the saddle, held his weight above the seat before he eased down. Sully's ears were flipping back and forward but the horse was rock still.

Blue sat, stuck that right boot in the stirrup, held his breath a moment, then ask more through a suggestion, a tightening of his legs rather than any kick or hard shove, and Sully walked forward like he was an ancient cowpony the boss kept in reserve when his kids came visiting from a far-away city.

EPILOGUE

His head rested on the seat of his saddle, he chewed on the last rind of bacon; salt-sweet and fatty and it went well with a biscuit broke in half and cooked in the left-over bacon grease. Where he could see him, Sully was hobbled since there wasn't a tree in sight, nothing but long blowing lines of high grass, hills that came in and out of each other like a weaving. Blue sky going gray to black, nighttime setting up with stars and coyotes singing off key and echoing. No cars or trains, no street lights or high buildings, nothing but clean air and quiet, and a good horse waiting on tomorrow's travel.

There was enough coffee left for the morning, and a few more biscuits. A woman, most likely Right's new bride, had sent along a tin of honey and Blue figured he'd treat himself to the sweet on that last biscuit before he rode out. It was a feast for him, better than anything he'd eaten for a while, except maybe for ribs and that rice in the dive, with Willie Simms for company.

Even his butt, his wounded pride, his grazed hindquarters packed with some kind of fancy ointment, even that part of him didn't hurt. There hadn't been a twinge when he first sat deep into his saddle; legs long and easy on the roan's hide, hands feeling the weight of the reins, the wet mouth holding the bit. All his senses and thoughts were wide open, testing, hearing, listening; eventually he rolled over on his good side, pulled down his hat and went to sleep.

Much later a coyote came up checking on the remains of the fire, the smell of grease hardening in the pan. Blue lay quiet, body tense; he knew exactly where he'd placed the rifle Con had left him, within easy grab. But he was curious.

The coyote stood and then stretched his head and neck out and his tongue took in a lick of grease. Another lick; Blue was smiling as the coyote took that last step so he could put his head down and clean out the pan. It was only when the coyote tried to take the pan with him that Blue sat up, yelled once and Sully whinnied, the coyote dropped the pan, barked and ran.

He'd been here before, this was his life; friend to hungry coyotes and curious ravens, and the commotion eased his spirit.

Blue took in that last deep breath before returning to sleep and the important world came back to him; the horse, his saddle, the coyote's scent, the wind carrying the aroma of sweet grass.

William A. Luckey

Made in the USA
Charleston, SC
19 August 2012